I0570979

The Elder Chronicles

Volume 8

Mutation

By

Robyn Kelly

This story is fiction. The settings are imaginary. Any resemblance of the characters or places to actual persons or places is purely coincidental.

Table of Contents

Prologue

Once again, the group of Elders gathered to hear Red Hawk explain another segment of their history. It had been ten years since the new Elders had come to live in the butte. To most of the earliest residents many of the events since then were common knowledge. But the earlier details were far and few between.

Rumors always circulated before each session as to what secrets would be revealed, what dangers had been averted, what great adventures had taken place. This time was no exception. The most prevalent rumor was that some great truth would be revealed. What that truth might be, no one knew.

At the appointed time, everyone who could, gathered in the south end of the valley. They patiently awaited the arrival of Red Hawk. Again, she was late. More rumors circulated through the crowd. Then, at last, she came through the opening into the valley. A strange silence came over the gathered Elders as she came into view.

Two things stood out. Her flaming red hair was more sparse and much duller than before and was also streaked with gray. It was still held back by a beaded head band. Her customary serape-style dress had been replaced by a wrap-around dress. It was tied at the waist and the waist tie still supported a knife sheath. She was still wearing her usual moccasins and had her medicine bag tied around her neck.

On this visit, however, she was also carrying a long totem stick. She was using it as an aid to walking as she moved over uneven ground. When she reached a spot in front of the crowd, she planted her stick into the sand and seemed to slide down it into her favored, cross-legged sitting position.

A hush came over the Elders, almost as much in shock at her appearance as in anticipation of her remarks. When all was quiet, she began …

"I am sad to report that there have been two deaths in the family. Two years ago, just after our last session, Gray Wolf died of cancer. We held a funeral in the eastern end of the reservation for all to attend, then a ritual death ceremony at the small butte where his body was cremated. Perhaps you saw the smoke from the funeral pyre.

"Last year, my husband Sam was fatally shot while investigating a case of fraud. His killer was subsequently arrested based on information Sam had uncovered. Sam's death was treated as the murder of a law enforcement officer and, thanks to our new and improved court proceedings, his killer is currently awaiting his own execution.

"Now, before I relate to you the latest adventures of your eastern sentinels, let me give you a brief history of the Elders prior to your arrival in the Butte.

"More than a thousand years ago, the original Elders were living in peace on a small planet many light years away from Earth. A hostile race suddenly threatened their planet. Having no means of defending against the invaders, the Elders elected to abandon their home world. The last ship to leave their planet was seen and chased by an enemy scout ship. During the chase, an escape pod containing a few of the Elders was jettisoned. That escape pod landed on the Earth in the vicinity of this butte. Due to help from a very unexpected source, the few Elders were able to conquer their pursuers and took up permanent residence in this butte.

"A thousand years later, their number had grown so great that the butte could no longer comfortably support them. They began sending out small groups to start other colonies among the humans. That proved, at the time, to be an unworkable plan. The humans rose up against the Elders, claiming that were unacceptable homosexuals, or worse. One couple attempted to start a small farm in Arkansas. The farm was successful and the couple mated before local bigots attacked the farm and burned it to the ground. One of the Elders managed to escape the fire with her child.

"Unfortunately, that Elder was accidentally killed before she could reach the safety of the butte. Her child survived. The human who killed her found the child and took it home with him. He and his wife attempted to raise the Elder child. That effort failed completely and the child escaped her captors just as she was reaching puberty.

"The child came to my attention while I was practicing clinical psychology at the Tucson hospital.

I recognized the child's unique properties and managed to turn her over to a Councilor from the Butte. When I tried to follow up on the child at a later date, I was told by Grey Wolf that only a shaman could interact with the Elders. I persisted and he agreed to train me to become a shaman. After months of grueling training, the tribe accepted me as a shaman and that allowed me to interact with the Elders. Since that date, I have been your protector.

"The child I mentored was called, Enela. As a young Elder she proved to be more than a handful for the Council. Her lack of an Elder childhood allowed her yen for exploration and adventure to prevail. She was the one who located the hidden alien scout ship and learned how it worked. She also befriended a human teenager whom she pressed into the service of the Elder community. When the Council learned of the capabilities of the alien craft, they hatched a plan to return all of the Elders to their original home world. (Believing that the alien threat was by now no longer viable.) To test their theory they sent a small group of Elders back in time to help the first Elders who had arrived on this planet. When that effort succeeded (as they knew it had to), they planned the final evacuation. Enela spent the night prior to the evacuation with her human friend.

"After the evacuation, Enela's friend Mary Gauss, discovered that she was pregnant. She used the income from a $300,000,000 lottery payout that Enela had left her to move to New Mexico. She named her child Joanne Elena and soon discovered that the child had more Elder attributes than human. Joanne came to my attention when she came to

Wakulla on a summer camp outing and passed out from the pain of puberty.

"After surviving puberty and returning to New Mexico, Elena, as she chose to call herself, felt the depressing loneliness of being the only remaining Elder on Earth. She concocted a plan to create new Elders, based on the artificial insemination process she had observed at her summer camp. You, my young Elders, are the result of that plan.

"You will recall that, after the last of you came to the valley, some of the more adept were dubbed sentinels and sent out to live among the humans to function as a sort of early warning system. They were to notify those in the butte if there was any news involving you or if any danger threatened you. They were also allowed to take action against the danger, should that prove necessary.

"This is the story of two of those sentinels."

Chapter 1

A Pleasant Day in DC

It was Tuesday. Naomi and Serina were lounging in their apartment on the west side of Washington, DC. When the sentinel program was first established, Naomi had asked specifically for Washington. She felt that this would ultimately be the most dangerous city for Elders. It was here that the laws were made. It was here that the national police agencies were based. Her foresight was about to bear fruit.

Naomi and Serina made a great team. They had first worked together to determine Elena's problem with the new Elders. Naomi could manipulate the human mind with the best of the Elders. Serina had an innate ability to manipulate electronic, electrical and mechanical devices. They had not yet officially become a couple, but all the Elders who knew them said that it was inevitable.

Unfortunately for Naomi's temperament, there had been nothing for her to do for the past several weeks. She was bored and looking for some distraction. So far, it didn't look like today was going to be any different.

Naomi was searching the daily gossip paper for something of interest, when her eyes spotted a unique story.

"Hey, Serina," Naomi called out. "This looks interesting."

"What?" Serina asked from the kitchen. She was looking for something to nosh on for lunch.

"Article in the newspaper," Naomi replied.

"That gossip rag you read?" Serina still was more interested in lunch.

"It's not a 'gossip rag'," Naomi retorted. "It's the daily version of the 'National Enquirer'. It prints all the really juicy news that the other papers won't touch because they are afraid of lawsuits."

"Exactly," said an already bored Serina.

"But this article is different," Naomi explained. "Come take a look."

Serina emerged from the kitchen nibbling on a piece of cheese. "Want some?" she teased Naomi.

"Later," Naomi persisted. "Take a look at this article." She held up the newspaper. "It's all about this person who was not hit by a bus."

"Each day there are thousands of people who are not hit by a bus," Serina groaned. "What makes this incident so special?"

"This person leaped out of the way, just in time," Naomi said, still waving the article.

"So, there are a hundred persons each day who are not hit by a bus because they leap out of the way," Serina was still nibbling on the cheese, but she did sit on the arm of Naomi's chair.

"Twenty feet out of the way?" Naomi asked, handing the paper to Serina.

"Hmm," Serina mumbled. "There is even a great picture of the bus. But that photo of the young girl leaves a lot to be desired. It's all blurry."

"I noticed," Naomi agreed. "Does that bring anything to mind?"

Serina spent a few minutes reading the short article and looking at the pictures. Naomi was right, she decided. There was something fishy about the event.

"A young girl jumps some twenty feet from a standing position to avoid being hit by a bus," Serina summarized. "And then a photographer can't seem to get a clear picture of her. It stinks. It was probably just concocted to spice up a slow news day."

"Maybe," Naomi hedged. "But, if you didn't want your picture taken, what would you do? I mean, other than busting up the photographer's camera."

"Well," Serina actually gave the question more thought than Naomi had intended, "I could tamper with the camera's settings. But that might become obvious if the photographer was paying attention. I could move or turn away. But he would know that I had done that and just keep trying. I might alter his vision so that he thought the image was clear when it really wasn't. That might work the best."

"Everything you suggested was something that an Elder could do," Naomi agreed. "But what could a human do that would be undetectable?"

"Nothing," was Serina's considered opinion.

"So," Naomi pressed the point, "why the blurred picture? Unless, it was the best they had."

"You think this was an Elder?" Serina asked.

"Let's find out," Naomi suggested. "Let's get on the Kaleidoscope and find out if there are any known Elders wandering around Washington.

"They are supposed to tell us if anyone is headed our way," Serina protested.

"Sure they are," Naomi teased. "Let's check anyway."

Serina walked over to their desk and used the Kaleidoscope program to contact the valley. She asked if there were any Elders visiting Washington, or if there were any Elders who were not accounted for. While she was waiting for a reply, she looked through their latest emails to see if she had missed a message. Whenever an Elder left the valley, the Council *was* supposed to advise each of the sentinels, just in case.

She found no advisory messages and soon the answer to her query came from the valley. No Elders visiting Washington and no one missing.

She informed Naomi of the situation, then asked, "Could Elena have missed any Elders?"

"We were there," Naomi answered. "The only ones we left behind were definitely human. I don't think any human could have carried this off?"

"Soooo?" Serina asked. She did not really want to consider the options.

"You read the last paragraph," Naomi said. "The 'authorities' took the young girl to a 'local hospital' to make sure she was alright. I'll bet they were as confused as we are and wanted more than just to insure her health."

"Road trip?" Serina asked

"I don't know," Naomi considered the various options. "What would we gain? Supposing that we could even find her based on the dearth of information in this article."

"True," Serina agreed. "We don't really know where she was taken, or how long they kept her. And if we start nosing around, we could attract more attention than we want to."

"Yeah," Naomi said, somewhat halfheartedly. "Maybe it would be better just to let the matter drop. After all, it could be a phony story at best or some sneaky trap at worst."

"You really want to check it out, don't you?" Serina knew Naomi all too well.

The two looked at each other for a few moments the said, in unison, "Road trip!"

"Okay," Serina said. "Where are we going and how?"

"The picture of the bus," Naomi pointed out, "shows a street sign for Constitution Ave. The article says she was taken to a local hospital, so why don't we start at Bridgeport Hospital? It's in the general location."

"Okay," Serina agreed, "How?"

"Ali," Naomi said.

Ali was a young cab driver, who Naomi and Serina had befriended shortly after they arrived in Washington. For a certain price, and the fun of the adventure, Ali was happy to help them with any of their transportation needs. He was a bit of a daredevil behind the wheel, but he knew the area well and was also dependable.

Naomi grabbed a cell phone from the desk and called Ali's number. He answered immediately.

"Ali, we need your services for about an hour. How soon can you meet us at Reservoir Rd and Wisconsin?" As a matter of safety, the two never met Ali at their home. The less he knew, the less he could reveal.

"15-20 minutes." Was Ali's terse answer.

"Okay."

"We'd better get dressed before we rush out the door," Serina suggested.

At home, Naomi and Serina usually wore no clothing. Now, the two quickly grabbed a couple of dresses and some shoes from the bedroom closet. Naomi also took a crisp $100 bill out of a desk drawer for Ali. Then the two left their apartment and headed for the designated meeting point.

Ali approached the intersection right on time, but from the wrong direction. He didn't let that bother him, he streaked through the intersection and did an immediate u-turn into on-coming traffic, coming to a screeching stop in front of Naomi and Serina.

"Where to?" he asked as soon as the two were inside the vehicle.

"Bridgeport Hospital", Serina said. Ali slammed the car in gear, and they were off.

Chapter 2

Hospital Visit

Bridgeport Hospital was one of the older facilities in Washington. It was three stories tall. It had red brick walls with wooden windows and well worn concrete steps. Inside it was not so much dirty as just well worn.

Naomi and Serina got out of the cab when Ali pulled up at the main entrance. Naomi paid Ali and told him that they would call if they needed him again. The two turned and walked up the steps into the hospital.

Inside the main entrance was a large lobby. In the center of the lobby was a large table with and 'Information' sign suspended from the front edge. A young woman in white pants, white blouse and green vest sat at the table behind a computer screen. A cloth badge on her vest identified her as a 'Bridgeport Volunteer'.

Naomi walked up to the table and said, "We're looking for the 'Jane Doe' they brought in yesterday, the one involved in the incident with the bus. We think she may be our sister. Can you tell us what room she is in?"

The young woman looked up at Naomi and Serina, reacted in a non-descript manner and typed the name on her keyboard. Then the three waited while the computer did its thing. "You did say,

'J-A-N-E—D-O-E'," the volunteer asked. And, when Naomi acknowledged that as correct, she replied, "Sorry, we don't seem to have anyone by that name in the hospital."

"Do you have any other resources?" Serina asked, somewhat hopefully.

"I do have a paper copy they print up for the night crew" the woman answered. She reached into a drawer and pulled out several pages that had been well used. She checked the list. Then she proclaimed, "Here is a reference to a Jane Doe. She is listed as being in room 323."

"How do we get there?" Naomi asked.

"Take the elevator over there," the young woman pointing to her right, "and follow the signs on the wall."

During this exchange, Serina had been watching the flow of people about the lobby area. For absolutely no reason, she asked the volunteer, "Do all volunteers wear green vests?"

"Oh, no," she responded. "The administrative volunteers, like me, wear green vests. The medical volunteers wear red and the nursing assistants wear blue."

"Come on!" Naomi called out impatiently as she headed for the elevator.

Once they got to the third floor, Naomi and Serina followed the signs on the wall to room 323. They paused for a second outside the door. It was only partially ajar. Both Naomi and Serina scanned the room for signs of life. They sensed none. Finally, Naomi pushed the door open and entered the room.

It was a single bed room with a small restroom near the head of the bed. The bed was empty; the bedding was taut and smooth. It was obviously made up for a new resident.

Naomi and Serina returned to the hallway and looked around. About thirty feet farther down the hall was what appeared to be a nurses' station. They headed in that direction. When they got there, they found the station deserted. That was all the invitation Serina needed.

"Back me up," she said and started browsing around the desks and papers. She checked the charts on the patients in residence. There was no mention of a Jane Doe. A nurse headed toward the station from the far end of the hall, but turned off into a patient's room.

Serina saw an 'out' basket and started leafing through it. Naomi saw the nurse leave the room she had entered and head toward the station. There was no apparent danger from the other direction, so she went out to meet the on-coming nurse.

"Excuse me," she said, "I am looking for the Jane Doe who was in room 323 yesterday. Can you help me?"

Naomi had obviously interrupted the nurse's train of thought. It took her a few seconds to refocus. "Jane Doe; Room 323" Naomi repeated.

"Oh," the nurse finally replied. "There was no one in that room when I came on duty this morning."

Naomi quickly checked. The nurse seemed to be quite sincere.

There followed a brief dance between Naomi and the nurse as the latter tried to get around Naomi and back to her station. Naomi ended up following the nurse. When they reached the station, it was empty.

Naomi kept going, searching for Serina. She found her in Room 323.

"It was the only space I knew would be safe," Serina explained when Naomi caught up with her.

"Did you find anything?" Naomi asked.

"You bet I did," Serina replied, "but you aren't going to like it. This was in the outbox."

Serina handed Naomi a single piece of paper. It was a patient transfer form.

"Oh, no" Naomi groaned. "Am I reading this correctly? Jane Doe was picked up just before midnight by an independent patient transfer company and taken to Walter Reed Medical Center?"

"That's how I read it," Serina agreed. "They came in just as the mid-night shift was coming on duty. A time of mass confusion. Picked her up with minimum documentation, possibly no authorization, and moved her out."

"As I recall," Naomi offered, "Walter Reed is a huge place. Many buildings, more offices. Does that paper give us any idea just where they took her?"

"Dream on!" Serina answered.

"You mean we're at a dead end?" Naomi was pissed.

"Not necessarily," Serina replied carefully. She folded the transport receipt and put it into her pocket. "Suppose we go talk to the hospital administration people."

Naomi and Serina went back to the elevator and rode down to the first floor. On exiting the elevator they looked around for a likely office. Nothing was obvious. They went back to the information desk. One inquiry there and they were directed toward the rear of the hospital. There they found the administrative suite.

Naomi spoke to the receptionist, "We would like to speak with the administrator concerning your loss of a patient."

"I'm sorry," she replied. "All of the administrators are currently busy. If you would like to leave you phone number, perhaps one of them could give you a call."

"They can meet with us right now," Naomi insisted, "or we'll give our information to a few news hounds we happen to know. These guys are like ravenous dogs with rabies when they get the scent of a good juicy scandal." Naomi accompanied her words with a little mental prodding.

"Please wait here a minute," the receptionist back-pedaled. She retreated into an inner office. In a moment she reappeared and escorted Naomi and Serina into the deputy administrator's office.

The man was seated behind his desk and did not bother to rise when Naomi and Serina entered his office. "What can I do for you?" he asked peevishly.

"You had a 'Jane Doe' patient in room 323 last night. She is no longer in this hospital. Yet there is no discharge record. Perhaps you can tell us what happened to her."

"Well, if she is no longer with us, I can assure you she was discharged …" Serina did not let him continue the thought.

"She was our sister!" Serina interjected. "If she had been properly discharged, she would have come home. We haven't seen her since yesterday morning. The newspaper said she was brought to this hospital after an accident with a bus; and there is a record that she was in room 323. We want to know where she is now."

"Let me make some inquiries," the administrator suggested. He picked up the phone and punched in an internal number. He spoke a few quiet words, waited for a few seconds, spoke some more words, waited a while longer, more words and a longer wait. Then he hung up.

"Well," he said at last, "it seems that she was here in the hospital yesterday.'

Naomi picked up on the ploy. "We know that!" she said quite forcefully. "We want to know where she is now!" She added a little mental nudge just to keep things on track.

"I am afraid," the administrator acknowledged, "that we just don't know at the moment." Then he quickly added before Naomi erupted again, "But we are working on that problem as we speak."

At that moment his phone rang and he grabbed for it. "Yes? ... Yes! ... Well, find out!"

He looked back at Naomi and Serina. "According to the charge nurse who was on duty in that ward last night, the 'Jane Doe' patient was transferred to Walter Reed Medical Center, because she needed care that we couldn't provide."

"Then you can produce a copy of the transfer receipt?" Serina asked.

"Of course," the director replied. There were more telephone calls. Several more calls. Naomi did a little more tweaking. After a few minutes, the administrator was sweating heavily.

"It appears," he finally said quite weakly, "that we can't find the transfer receipt at the moment."

"Look," Naomi persisted, "you are the head of a prominent hospital. Surely, if you actually transferred a patient to another hospital, you can get a confirmation from that hospital." She simultaneously made that idea seem quite attractive.

The administrator picked up the phone again, told his secretary to connect him to Walter Reed. "Turn on the speaker," Serina insisted.

Several clicks later there were a few questions, some explanations, a transfer or two. Naomi and Serina were listening intently for some hint as to where Jane Doe might have ended up. At last, a clerk at the Naval Support Facility acknowledged that they had received the patient.

"Bingo!" thought Naomi and Serina simultaneously. Naomi immediately erased the entire incident from the administrator's mind and she and Serina left his office. He was left speaking on the phone with a person he did not know about a topic he couldn't remember.

Naomi and Serina left the hospital. They walked over to the nearest Metro station and rode back to the west end. They then had a short walk to their apartment. They had a lot to think over.

Chapter 3

Bethesda

When Naomi and Serina got back to their apartment, they had a bite to eat and continued their discussion of what to do next. Naomi wanted to go directly to the medical center right then and there. Serina called for a little more restraint and planning.

"Look at it this way, Naomi," she explained her position. "We only know that she was taken to the Navy Support Facility at the Walter Reed Medical Center. We don't know whether she is still there. Even if she is, we don't know anything about the facility or where in the facility she is. We really need a plan before we just go barging in there. Personally, I don't want to find her by being locked in the same cell she is in."

"Okay," Naomi finally ceded. "We need a plan. Let's start at the beginning and work our way through it. I say we need to get there as soon as possible. We don't know how long they will keep her there or how long she can withstand persistent probing by experts."

"Probing?" Serina asked.

"Yes!" Naomi persisted. "Why do you think they took her in the first place. She wasn't even hit by the bus. She wasn't 'injured' at all. The trip to Bridgeport was probably just precautionary because it was convenient. But the transfer to the Navy hospital had to be intentional, most likely so that they could examine her in more detail. Not for her injuries, but for her abilities."

"Alright," Serina agreed. "She's probably in some danger and speed would be good. Let's assume we get there, then what? Just sneaking in and searching the place clandestinely would take hours and there is a high probability we would be caught. I can't instantly disarm all their surveillance equipment. I don't even know what or how much they have."

"So," Naomi was thinking out loud, "We need to be sneaky. Suppose we concoct a story and walk in without trying to hide. You handle the locks and cameras as may be necessary and I'll handle the people. As for the story – we're two consultants from out of town who were asked to look at Jane Doe and render an opinion."

"Better yet, out of country," Serina offered. "You know a little German, don't you?" Naomi nodded. "And Germany is about 6 hours ahead of us – so, if we arrive at midnight, fresh off the plane, … "

"Great!" Naomi insisted. "Call Ali and have him pick us up at eleven. What clothes do we have that look German?"

"But, if we find Jane Doe, how do we get out of there?" Serina wanted more details.

"We'll make that up as we go. Our first problem is just to get in undetected and find her."

Ali, as usual, appeared exactly on time. When Naomi told him they were going to Walter Reed complex in Bethesda, Maryland, he didn't even blink. He just took off like a rocket and in forty-five minutes they were at the outer gate.

When the gate guard questioned them, Naomi simply said they were going to the Naval Support Facility and added a little extra prompt. The guard waved them through. Ali drove past the main complex to a smaller building on the north side of the road. The Naval Support facility was a modern two-story building on the left side of the road. It did not at all seem intimidating. Ali turned into the driveway and stopped at the main entrance. Naomi told Ali to find an unobtrusive parking spot nearby and to wait for her call. She also told him, when they called, to come back to the driveway and park just beyond the door, out of view.

The lobby was well lit and Naomi could see a guard desk situated at the back. Naomi and Serina walked to the door. It was locked, so Serina knocked on it to get the guard's attention. She could see the guard look up, then the door lock clicked and the door opened.

Naomi and Serina walked through the door and over to the desk. Serina noted the type of lock on the door and the location of the video monitors.

"What is your business here, tonight?" the guard asked.

"*Wir sind schon auf Deutschland gekommen. Ach! Entshuldigen.* Pardon me. We just flew in from

26

Germany," Naomi explained with a heavy German accent. "We were asked to come here to consult on the Jane Doe case. I am Dr. Wermutt, a psychiatrist; and this is Dr. Allers, who is a noted parapsychologist. We would like to see the patient immediately, we have to catch a plane back to Germany at noon tomorrow."

"Now?" the guard wasn't impressed.

"*Ja!* Yes, now!" Naomi replied. We spent our 'night' sleeping on the plane. It is now our 'morning' and we are ready to get to work. Would you be pleased to tell us where the Jane Doe patient is."

With this last statement, Naomi urged the guard very strongly to issue the necessary passes without any further enquiries. The guard complied and soon Serina and Naomi each had their pass.

"*Und, wo ist* ... the location of our patient?" Naomi repeated.

The guard consulted a computer screen hidden below the top edge of his counter. "Take the elevator," he pointed to his right, "down to level 3. The nurses' station will be down the corridor to your right when you exit the elevator."

Naomi and Serina thanked the guard and followed his instructions. "Interesting building," Naomi thought out loud, "Two stories above ground, three below ground." To Serina, she whispered, "Note everything that might be dangerous to us."

When they got off the elevator on level 3, Naomi noted the entrance to a stairwell opposite the elevator. There was an 'EXIT' sign on the ceiling pointing to it. Then the two turned down the corridor toward the nursing station.

As Naomi had expected, the nurses had just changed shifts. The station was in a mild state of confusion. Naomi pulled the same story with one of the nurses as she had with the guard. It had the same effect. The nurse led the pair back down the hall to room number L3-45. She used her pass to unlock the door to the room and ushered the two 'doctors' inside.

"Thank you so much," Naomi told the nurse. "We will use the call button if we need further assistance." The nurse hesitated for a moment, then she left the room and returned to the nursing station.

Serina gently indicated the video camera in the corner of the room behind her and silently mouthed the word 'audio'. In a second, Serina said, "Audio scrambled."

Naomi surveyed the room. It was a typical hospital room: small bathroom, tray table, bed, trash can, cabinets with counter top and sink, small wardrobe closet. There was no obvious large mirror in the wall, which might indicate surveillance from an adjoining room.

"Let's get to work", she said.

Naomi went over to the bed. "I know you are awake," she said quietly. "You woke up when we came in. My friend and I are here to get you out of this place. It would help greatly if you would cooperate – just a little bit."

Jane Doe remained still, feigning sleep.

"Take a good look at me," Naomi persisted, as she unzipped the front of her dress. "We're just like you. And if you don't cooperate we're going to be stuck here in a bed, just like you are."

Jane Doe barely cracked her eyes. She squinted at Naomi.

"See," Naomi said as she gently lifted the front of her wig. "Sparse hair, white skin, not quite five feet tall."

This time Jane Doe did take a good look. She struggled to turn over toward Naomi, but was hindered by wrist restraints on both arms. "You will really get me out of here?" she asked pleadingly.

"That's our plan," Naomi said. "But you have to trust us, and cooperate." She replaced her wig, combing it out with her fingers, and zipped her dress. "Once we start taking action, things are going to pop. Can you walk?"

"Yes, I think so," Jane Doe responded. "They have kept me in bed for two days. I may be a little weak. What can I do to help?"

"Just follow orders," Naomi prompted. "We may not have time to repeat them." Then she turned to Serina. "I'm going to call the nurse. As soon as she walks in the door, scramble the video."

Naomi walked over to the bed and pressed the call button, which was conveniently hanging just out of Jane Doe's reach. Then she positioned herself behind the door and waited for the nurse. While they were waiting, she briefed Serina on the rest of the plan.

In a few minutes, the nurse arrived and entered the room. Naomi instantly cut off her vocal ability and pushed the door closed. Serina killed the video and also disabled the nurse's communicator.

Naomi immediately freed Jane Doe from her restraints. The instant she was free she made a bee line for the restroom. Then, Naomi convinced the nurse to remove all of her clothes. The scrubs, shoes and cap she threw on the bed for Jane Doe. The rest she put in the metal waste basket.

When Jane Doe returned from the restroom, smiling contentedly, Naomi told her to take off her hospital gown and put on the nurse's scrubs, shoes and hat. While Jane was occupied, Serina and Naomi put the hospital gown on the nurse and strapped her in the bed once occupied by Jane Doe and covered her with the sheet.

Then they took a few minutes to look at their work. Naomi retrieved the nurse's id badge. "Okay," she said, "This is it!. We're all going to walk out the door together. Jane you stay between us and keep quiet – no matter what happens. Just walk unless we say otherwise. Once we get outside the building, there will be a taxi waiting for us. Serina, as soon as we pass through a door, secure it behind us. Scramble any video surveillance equipment you locate. Is everyone ready?"

The other two nodded. Naomi pulled the waste basket into the center of the room, under the fire sensor in the ceiling, crammed in some paper towels on top of the clothing, added a small amount of an alcohol based fluid she had found on the counter and set it on fire with a match, brought for just that purpose.

Serina sent out a call to Ali, telling him to get in place. Then she opened the door and check ed the hallway. It was empty. She waved her arm forward and the three set off. Once through the door, Naomi took the lead as Serina scrambled the lock on the door of the room. Then the three moved down the hall at a fast walk. As Naomi came upon a fire alarm switch on the wall, she pulled it. Sirens sounded, lights flashed and the three hurried on toward the stairwell.

The door to the stairwell was unlocked and the three headed up to the first floor and freedom, they hoped. They made it to level 2 without a hitch. Then a few others joined behind them on the stairs. No one bothered them so they continued. There were others using the stairs at level 1, but still no one seemed to pay any attention to the three escapees.

Down on level 3, the nurses had responded to room L3-45, but they couldn't get into the room. The lock was somehow malfunctioning. One of the nurses finally thought of calling the guard station for help. An armed guard responded from somewhere on the floor and used his weapon to shoot the lock off the door. When they got inside, the nurses found the room full of smoke. The sprinkler in the center of the room was still spewing water over everything.

One nurse got to the bed without slipping on the wet floor. When she saw who was in the bed, she let out a shriek and told another nurse by the door to notify the guards that Jane Doe had escaped.

By that time Naomi and her party were already on the first floor and on their way out the door. It had been unlocked when the fire alarm sounded to permit building residents to get to safety. Naomi led her group toward Ali's waiting taxi. When they reached it, the three quickly piled in and Naomi told Ali, "Get us out of here, now!"

Ali didn't waste time. In a few seconds, he was on the road out of the center. Serina had to remind him to take it easy going out the gate. No sense in attracting attention at this stage.

Naomi and Serina watched carefully to see if they were being followed, but saw no sign of any trailing vehicle. They did, however, pass several emergency vehicles going the opposite direction. They stopped at the guard house, dropped off the vehicle pass and turned onto the main highway south.

In less than an hour, Ali dropped them back in the vicinity of their apartment. Naomi paid Ali for his services, then she took a moment to erase the entire incident from Ali's mind.

Chapter 4

Divina's Story

Once back at the apartment, the first order of business was a good night's sleep – at least what was left of it. Jane Doe and Naomi awoke in the morning to the aroma of frying eggs and bacon. Serina and Naomi had returned all of their clothes to the closet, but 'Jane' was still wearing the nurse's scrubs. Eventually, all three gathered around the breakfast bar and made the food disappear. Then it was time to get down to business.

"Well, Miss Jane Doe," Naomi began, "you are free to leave any time you'd like; but I do wish you would stick around awhile and answer a few questions."

"Questions?" 'Jane' asked tentatively.

"Like we told you last night," Serina tried to ease her anxiety, "we are just like you. We thought we knew all of the others like ourselves. But you are someone new. We would really like to know where you came from so we can figure out how you came about. Or is that too convoluted?"

"No," 'Jane' replied. "I get your meaning. I think I am just as confused. I guess, after what I've been through, I am still a bit cautious. Just what is it you want to know?"

"For starters," Naomi offered, "What is your name? This 'Jane doe' business is getting a little old."

"Oh, of course," 'Jane was somewhat relieved, "My name is, Divina Wilson."

"That's bad news for 'starters'," Naomi moaned.

"Why bad news?" Divina sounded worried.

"Our names do end in an 'ah' sound," Serina explained, "but we don't use any of the 'hard' consonants, like 'd', 't', 'g', 'k', you know. And we never use a 'last name'. Despite the fact that you are short, have white skin, black eyes and sparse hair, it is highly unlikely that you are really one of us."

"Who is 'we' and 'us?'" Divina asked.

Naomi and Serina exchanged glances. Then Naomi gave one of those shrugs that said, "I can undo this later if I have to."

"We are called 'Elders'", Naomi said. "We came from a place far away a long time ago. A few members of our community, such as Serina and I, are scattered around the country as 'sentinels' to watch out for the others. Let's see if we have any record of you."

Naomi went over to the computer and called up the Kaleidoscope.

"Wow!", Divina exclaimed. "That is one beautiful screen saver."

"It does other things," Serina said, as Naomi logged in and sent a message out to everyone asking if there was any 'Divina' in the records. The answers came back almost immediately. 'No such person.'

"It seems I have already told you more than I should have," Naomi admitted. "Now we really do need to know more about you. Will you let me examine you – I promise I won't touch you in the process? Just stretch out here on the floor."

Divina somewhat reluctantly complied. Naomi knelt down on the floor beside her and began passing her hands over Divina's body, from the head to the crotch. Then she looked at the soles of her feet and motioned her to expose her palms.

"May I feel for a pulse?" Naomi asked.

"I really think I am alive," Divina said somewhat pointedly.

"So am I," Naomi said. "Feel my pulse." She held out her wrist. Divina felt, felt again, then she looked up quite frightened.

Naomi held her hand out toward Divina's wrist. Divina acquiesced. Naomi felt her wrist, then she felt for a carotid pulse and a femoral pulse in rapid succession.

Serina looked inquisitively at Naomi. Naomi just shook her head.

Serina decided that it was time for her to enter the fray. "Alright, Divina," she said, "we know you have our appearance and our physiology. What about mental abilities? Have you ever been able to influence human activity?"

"A polite way of saying it," Divina replied.
"Yes, a few times. And to answer your next question, I was not sufficiently sure of my abilities to attempt trying to escape my captors. To be honest, they scared me."

"Divina, I originally told you that you could leave any time you wanted, and I will still stand by that; but I would really appreciate you filling in the gaps before you go. What can you tell me of your family history?"

"I guess I owe you that much," Divina said. "What do you want to know?"

"Your parents?" Naomi asked.

"My mother is, Francine Clancy," Divina answered. "My father is Ted Wilson. They were married in 2012, shortly after she graduated from high school. I was born a year later. My father is a real estate developer. We live in upstate New York. I am an only child, so far. I went to parochial school. I came to Washing to find a good government job. I wasn't looking and the bus surprised me. Anything else?"

"Well, that is a bit to digest all at once," Serina confessed. "Give us a few minutes."

"Your parents are Catholics?" Naomi ventured.

"Yes," Divina said, wondering what that had to do with anything.

"Have you ever heard of St. Thomas Academy?" Naomi continued her line of thought.

"Oh, yes," Divina explained. "My mother graduated from St. Thomas. She wanted me to go there, too; but I wanted to go somewhere closer to home."

"Bingo!" Serina exclaimed. Naomi immediately 'shushed' her before she could give away anything else. Divina glanced at the two of them in total confusion.

"Divina, you have put up with us for far too long," Naomi said. "It is high time you were off on your own again."

"She can't go off in those dirty scrubs," Serina scolded. "Divina, why don't you go in our room and select some smart outfit. I'll get you some money to make up for any you lost. I do suggest that you dye your hair, at least for a while. Even if the government doesn't know who you are, they probably took pictures of you that aren't blurred, and I'm sure they will be looking for you. You don't want to make it too easy for them."

"Yes," Serina agreed. "And next time, use your abilities to take them out before they get their hands on you. Now go get dressed."

Divina graciously accepted the clothes and the money offered. With many thanks, she left the apartment. As she went, Naomi called out behind her, "And watch out for busses!"

After Divina had left, Serina and Naomi sat down to consider the situation.

"So what do we know," Naomi asked, "and what does it all mean?"

"We know that Francine, Divina's mother, was a senior at St. Thomas Academy when Elena and her mother were there impregnating the seniors."

"Well, obviously, Divina wasn't the child Elena created, " Naomi offered. "She came 'a couple of years' later".

"But two humans have never created an Elder child." Serina persisted. "Francine wasn't an Elder; and there are no Elder males."

Silence reigned. Neither Serina nor Naomi wanted to be the one who broached the only possibility left. Eventually, Naomi gave in.

"It appears that the Elder gene is the more dominant," she said. "It also seems that it modified the mother's DNA. Is that even possible?"

"If it happened, it's possible," said the ever-dependable Serina.

"Do you realize the potential magnitude of this situation?" Naomi asked, as though she had just thought of it. "Two hundred young women walking around somewhere, any one of which could pop out another Elder child at any time. And what if those Elder children retain the gene?"

"The thought is overwhelming!" Serina emoted placing the back of her hand on her forehead.

"Seriously," Naomi suggested, "I think this is a question for the Council to decide. Let's give them a call before it's too late."

Chapter 5

Working Out The Details

Before calling the Valley, Naomi and Serina sat down and went over their options. There were only four possibilities that they could come up with: isolate all the St Thomas graduates and their children who might be effected, sterilize them, kill them, or protect them.

They immediately ruled out just killing them. Elders don't kill.

They decided that isolating them, assuming they could all be found, would not be a viable solution. There are potentially more of them now than there are Elders. The where and how of the isolation option were just too daunting.

Serina was in favor of finding them and sterilizing them. That would be simple and permanent. Until Naomi pointed out that they had a good head start, and that sterilization would be a slow solution. It would take time to find them all. The 'solution' might leak out and a resistance movement might form. It would not be a good situation.

That left just one alternative: protect them. Naomi and Serina just looked at each other. How in the world could they protect these people from the whole US government? There weren't enough sentinels – piff!, there weren't enough Elders.

"Wait a minute," Serina suddenly erupted. "Why don't we use the whole US government to protect *them*?"

Naomi was stopped dead in her thoughts. "Tell me more," was all she could muster.

"Well, we are assuming the government wants to capture us so they can probe into who or what we are. Not an unreasonable assumption, based on what we have seen so far."

"Get to the point," Naomi was tired of facing an insoluble problem.

"We simply invalidate that assumption," Serina said. "We convince the government that harassing Elders is a losing proposition."

"Isn't that a little easier said than done?" Naomi asked, in complete disbelief.

"I didn't say it would be easy," Serina responded. "But why don't we try to figure out how it *can* be done? After all, we are sitting here in the center of all the government's power. All we have to do is figure out how to control it. That should be right up your alley."

"Hmm," Naomi was cogitating. "Power, Control." She began pacing back and forth deep in thought.

"There are three centers of government power in Washington:" Naomi finally said. "The Supreme Court, The Congress and the President. I think we can rule out the Supreme Court. Their only power resides in controlling the other two.

"The Congress can enact laws to govern the people, but those laws have to be enforced by other powers. The only coercive power the Congress actually has is their little police force. It only controls the happenings within the Capital Building.

"That leaves the President. The President, as head of the Executive Branch of government, actually controls not only the military, but every national police force the country has. If we control the President, we control all he national police. The only question remaining is, How do we control the President?"

"You just get into the Oval Office and do your thing," Serina suggested. "Voila! We control the President."

"No good," Naomi protested. "Too many people under him in authority. If the President started acting irrationally, in their opinion, they would just ignore him until he could be replaced.

"We need something that will not only control the President, but all those in power under him." Then Naomi began pacing and thinking again. Five minutes later she stopped.

"I think I've got it!" she said triumphantly. "All we have to do is get the President to issue an order that is not only binding on him and his successors, but also on all, or most, of the people under him. Then we can just sit back and enforce it. After a few very prominent enforcements, everyone should fall into line."

"Brilliant!" Serina conceded. "But how do we put such an order in place?"

"We simply pay the President a visit," Naomi stated. "But we had better get the Council's approval before we attempt it. They may have to find replacements for us if we fail."

Serina agreed and went over to the computer to send out an emergency message. Then she turned to Naomi, "What do I say? Do I just tell them we want to control the President?"

"No, just tell them to get Elena and the Council together and give us a call." Naomi said.

The message went out at two o'clock, eleven o'clock Valley time. The return call came at almost four. Naomi and Serina used VOIP for their voice communications, as did the Valley. They gathered around their computer and turned up the volume.

Elena was the first to speak. She identified herself and said the Council members were present and listening. Naomi briefed them on the situation in Washington and the decision that she and Serina had come up with.

Several options were discussed. One of the Council members even suggested letting the government have the mothers and daughters. She said they weren't true Elders and their capture would have little impact on the rest of the Elders in the Valley. Serina had a more practical approach.

"Suppose we let the government have the mothers and daughters," Serina said. "If they get thorough about it, they may decide to continue the project. I imagine, if they persist they could even start a selective breeding program of their own. If they were successful we could one day find ourselves facing an opposing army of people just like us – or, perhaps, even better than us. If it went that far we would definitely be on the losing side.

"I agree," Elena said. "I think we ought to be proactive in this. If we stop it now, maybe we'll get a short breather before they start something else. How do you propose to do it, Naomi?"

"At the moment," Naomi answered, "I only have a vague idea. From what I have learned about the government, it runs on orders and regulations. I propose that we draft a regulation, that will be binding upon the President and his subordinates in the Executive Branch, and that will prohibit the harassment of Elders under some severe penalty. I would like to apply it to everyone, but that might be impractical. I suggest limiting its range to, for example, captains and above in the military and the equivalent in civilian and contractor forces."

"Civilian contractors?" one of the Councilors asked.

"Yes," Naomi said. "You would be surprised how many police type functions are already being handled by contractors. I also don't want to give them an out by omitting anyone."

"How do you plan to enforce such a regulation? Elena asked.

"By a severe fine and prison sentence," Serina inserted, "without benefit of trial or appeal. And in exceptional cases by Elder-administered justice."

"Will that be enough to deter the humans?" Elena asked. "They are known to be a zealous and adversarial people."

"I think some judicious applications of Elder justice following the first few violations will get the message across," Naomi mused. "I seem to recall stories of how you and a certain bird handled the FBI a few years back." Naomi and Serina could hear some questions being asked on the other end of the call.

"Okay," Elena said. "Stand by. We'll consider the solution."

The line went dead. Naomi and Serina looked at each other. If the Council didn't buy this approach, neither of them had a ready alternative. Although, Serina did happen to think Japan would be an interesting place to live.

Some ten minutes later, the computer indicated an incoming call. It was brief. The Chief Councilor simply told Serina and Naomi to implement their plan. They were to report back when it was up and working.

The two sat down and started planning. They decided to format the model as an executive directive. Their were dozens of different formats among the various government offices. They could let the various offices reformat the directive later.

Then they worked out the structure of the directive. The basic directive would establish the rules of engagement, two different certification sheets, a briefing sheet and the penalties for violating the directive. When they finished, this is what they had written.

The Rules of Engagement: Executive Directive X-101

1. (U) This directive applies to the Executive Branch of the Government of the United States of America and to all of the various elements of the Branch: military and civilian. It is binding upon all personnel, military, civilian and contractual, in grades GS-12/O-3 and above to include the President, Vice-President and all appointees throughout the Branch.

2. (S) Once annually every member of the Executive Branch, as defined above, will be briefed on the content of the Briefing Sheet. The Annual Briefing will begin on the first day of the fiscal year and be completed within thirty days. New personnel arriving in an agency between annual briefings will be briefed within one week of reporting for duty.

3. (S) Every person being briefed will sign an Individual Certification Form at the end of the briefing, acknowledging and accepting responsibility for the requirements of Directive X-101. This form will be retained by the individual's superior until it is replaced by a new Certification at the next Annual Briefing. If an individual has no supervisor, he or she will sign and retain the individual certification as a matter of record.

4. (S) Following the Annual Briefing, Every supervisor will prepare a Certification Summary Form listing the name of each individual under his/her personal control who was briefed. He will

then sign the Certification Summary Form and send it to his immediate superior.

5. (S) The President and Vice President will be personally briefed and will sign an Individual Certification Form. The President will receive an Individual Certification Form from the Vice-President, from each Secretary/Department head and from the Chief of the Joint Chiefs and a Individual Certification Form or Certification Summary Form from any special appointees, including members of his/her personal support staff.

6. (S) Failure to disseminate this directive in accordance with the provisions of paragraph 5 above will be deemed a violation of this directive.

7. (S) There is a single penalty for violating any aspect of this directive: a fine of $100,000.00 and a prison sentence of 50 years. This penalty will be enforced upon any positive evidence of a violation, intentional or otherwise. There will be no trial and no appeal is permitted. In cases of a grievous violation a special penalty may be invoked in accordance with the provision outlined on the Briefing Sheet.

8. (S) This directive, including the Briefing Sheet is classified Top Secret, No Foreign Dissemination and will be controlled under the codeword: Cosmic. Without the Briefing Sheet it will be classified Secret, No Foreign Dissemination and will be controlled under the codeword: Cosmic. Personnel being briefed will be granted access to Cosmic material for the purpose of the briefing.

The Briefing Sheet: Directive X-101:

1. (TS) There exist within the territory of the United States of America a small group of extra-terrestrials known as "The Elders". The Elders have lived clandestinely in this country for over 1000 years. They are peaceful and present no danger to human life. It is therefore ordered without reservation that, should you encounter an Elder, you will do nothing to hinder the Elder's activity or to harass the Elder in any way. They are to be completely ignored unless they specifically ask you for assistance. In such case you will immediately offer appropriate aid. Should an Elder be injured or killed, you will do nothing without the specific direction of another Elder. In the case of a deceased Elder, you will not touch the body, but cover it or hide it from view and protect the area from other humans.

2. (TS) Elders may be distinguished by the following characteristics: They are humanoid, between four and five feet in height. They have a pure white skin, black eyes, are hairless or have sparse black hair. Some have retractable scales on their palms and soles. They do not have a discernable pulse at the neck, wrist or groin. As a defensive measure they are able to manipulate human activity. Elders may, or may not wear clothing.

3. (TS) You will at no time make any mention of the material in this briefing. You will not refer to the

existence of the Elders or make any comments concerning the existence of extra–terrestrials. If you are asked about any possibility of such a situation, you will deny any knowledge of it without further comment.

4. (TS) In the case of serious violations of this regulation, Elders may invoke a special penalty in lieu of fine and prison time suggested in the base directive. Such action will be at their discretion.

5. (TS) No attempt will ever be made to locate or directly contact the Elder community.

6. (S) The prohibitions and penalties inherent in this briefing will be imposed upon you for the rest of your life, even if you should leave government service.

"Now that we have something to talk about," Serina said, as she examined the finished product, "what do we do with it?"

"Well," Naomi suggested, "It's not doing us any good here. I guess we had better get it implemented. Ready for a road trip?"

"Where and when?" Serina asked.

"Early tomorrow morning," Naomi answered. "The White House."

"Is the President even in residence at the moment?" Serina was ever the pessimist.

"Let's check," Naomi said as she called up a browser and checked the President's schedule. "Yes, for the rest of the week," she announced.

They were ready for the next step.

Chapter 6

Good Morning, Mr. President

As they were eating breakfast the next morning, Serina brought up the next obvious question.

"How are we going to get there? Limo, Ali, bus, Metro?"

"Personally," Naomi said, "I would really like a limo. Most limo drivers around here know how to get into the White House. But that might be a bit excessive. Ali knows his way around town, but I would bet he has never been to the White House. Besides, it would take a long time to get his beat up old taxi inspected and onto White House grounds. Bus and Metro are just too plebian for such a momentous occasion."

"Okay,' Serina said, "You've convinced me. We rent a town car. I'll make the call. You dig up some appropriate clothes."

So, decked out in simple, but colorful, dresses, the two Elders climbed into the back seat of a black town car and headed to the White House. It was starting out as a clear sunny day, cool and crisp.

"Where to?" the driver asked as he pulled away from the curb.

"West entrance of the White House, off Pennsylvania Avenue," Naomi directed. "We have a 10 o'clock appointment with the President." It is unknown what the driver thought of that particular statement, as he was well trained not to comment on his passengers' comments facially or verbally.

Promptly at nine thirty, the driver pulled up at the first checkpoint. The driver lowered his window and gave the guard Naomi's message. When the guard asked for names and passes, the driver gave the names from his order as Naomi and Serina Elder. The guard consulted his list of the day's visitors. He could find no such names and said so. From the backseat, Naomi suggested that he check again. She also added a little extra encouragement. The guard discovered his error and waved them through.

They drove slowly along the driveway to the portico where they encountered another guard post. Naomi didn't wait for the formalities, she just encouraged the guard to pass them to the door. There were two other cars in front of them and another coming from the rear. The President was going to have a busy day.

They got out at the door and sent the driver on his way. They had to stop and get a visitor's pass on the way inside. Naomi kept encouraging the guards. There were no difficulties. Naomi also nudged Serina indicating that she should start checking out the surveillance equipment.

There were several people milling about the lobby, discussing the day's business and the status of the local golf courses. Naomi and Serina made their way to the left side of the room and into the press hallway. Serina helped with the locks and alarms as necessary. At the other end of the hall they turned right and stepped into the presidential secretary's office.

"We have a ten o'clock appointment with the President," Naomi announced as she nudged the president's secretary to agree. Two or three more people came into the office. Naomi and Serina edged closer to the door of the Oval Office.

Naomi swept the Oval Office to determine how many people were inside. Apparently the President was alone. It was nearly ten and that was close enough. Neither Naomi nor Serina knew what the proper protocol was, but Naomi decided it was time to act. She motioned for Serina to clear any locks and the two slipped quietly through the door. Serina immediately disabled all surveillance systems.

The President looked up when the door opened, but could see nobody. He presumed someone was just looking in to see what was up. Several of his senior visitors did that when they became tired of waiting. He checked the clock on his desk and noted that it was indeed time to start receiving visitors. He sighed and reached over to press the button to notify his secretary that he was ready.

"That won't be necessary, Mr. President." Naomi said from the side of the room. The President started and immediately ran his eyes around the room in search of the speaker.

"My friend and I are right here," Naomi said, as she released her hold on the President's mind. The President stared when the two Elders 'miraculously' appeared before him.

"Just who are you and what are you doing in my office?" He demanded.

"We came to see you about a very important matter," Naomi explained. "As far as your secretary knows, we have a ten o'clock appointment."

"According to my calendar," The President said, squinting his eyes at his desk calendar, "my first appointment today is with Senator Black."

"What we have to say is much more important, and more interesting, than anything Senator Black may have had to offer. I suggest that you officially clear your calendar for a couple of hours. That way, your secretary will not be interrupting us. And I'm sure you know how testy some of those big-wigs can get when they have to wait."

As Naomi was speaking, the President slowly moved his hand beneath his desk and pressed his panic button. He did not know who these two idiots were, but he was sure he wanted to be rid of them.

In less than thirty seconds the doors burst open and several armed guards rushed in – only to find the President sitting calmly at his desk, alone. They all looked around for the source of the problem, but could see nothing. For that matter, neither could the President.

"Sorry, boys," the President said somewhat embarrassed, "my leg must have hit the button by mistake. Thanks for the prompt response."

The guards looked around again and, seeing no threat, retreated back to their stations. After they had exited the office, the President looked around again, shook his head and was about to summon his next appointment when Naomi spoke up again.

"We're over here now," she said from a position next to the windows. "Now, let's get one thing straight. We came here to speak with you on a very important matter. We are not going away until we do. You have seen what happens when you press your panic button. If you persist in that activity, your security people will have you locked up as being loony.

"If you have any other thoughts, we are perfectly ready to take other, more drastic measures, such as preventing you from moving if you try to get up and run, or to render you mute if you try to yell or scream.

"Are you prepared to discuss our matter at this time?"

The President thought for a few seconds before committing. Then he decided that he had little other choice. His visitors did not seem to be dangerous, and he was extremely curious as to their strange abilities. Perhaps, he thought, they are very adept hypnotists.

"Alright," the President said, "What is this urgent matter?"

While he had been thinking, Serina and Naomi had slipped out of their dresses. When the President looked up, they were standing there naked. He was flabbergasted.

"Our position is very simple, Mr. President," Serina said. We are not human. We are Elders. Our predecessors have been hiding on this planet for over 1000 years. Our numbers are growing and it is imperative that we begin leaving our hiding place and come out into human society.

"We present no danger to any humans and have no evil intent; we simply want to live our lives free from unwanted intrusion by human beings. Recently, one of our number was captured and spirited away to the Walter Reed Hospital complex, where she was held incommunicado, shackled to her bed.

"We managed to learn what happened to her and we freed her with only minor damage to the room, the loss of a few pieces of lingerie and the embarrassment of a nurse. What might have happened to her if we had not interceded is to horrible to contemplate.

"We can deal with local police forces. They have neither the resources nor the manpower to cause us much grief. The federal government is another matter entirely. They have the resources and power to totally destroy our entire community, should they have a mind to. That is what we have come her today to address."

Naomi took a copy of their regulation out of the folder she was carrying and placed it on the President's desk. "We are asking you to endorse this regulation and to direct its immediate implementation throughout the Executive Branch." Serina and Naomi had been standing in front of the President's desk. After placing the papers on the desk, they took seats on either side of the desk. The President looked quizzically between the two of them.

Naomi picked up on his thought. She simply said, "We don't leak."

The President didn't know whether to laugh, cry or scream, so he did nothing. He reached for the two pages and pulled them toward him. It took him a few minutes to read the proposal. He paused several times to digest what he was reading. Then he looked up.

"Do you really expect me to completely tie the hands of our entire police and military functions while you run around robbing, raping, pillaging and murdering at will?" The President exclaimed.

"In the first place," Naomi responded haughtily, "we do not rape or pillage or murder! Those are entirely human traits. Secondly, if you implement this directive, you can always cancel it at any time in the future, should it prove unwise or unworkable. We cannot stop you from doing that. Such action would, however, be at your own peril; in accordance with the penalty provisions."

A buzzer on the President's desk sounded. The President switched on the intercom and said, "Yes, Angela?" Serina tensed, ready to switch everything off in half a heartbeat.

"Your appointments are backing up, Mr. President." came from the speaker.

"Cancel all my morning appointments," the President replied, and shut off the intercom.

He drummed his fingers lightly on the desk, as if it helped him to think. Then he looked from one Elder to the other and stopped by chance on Naomi.

"I presume you have thought about implementing this," he said. What did you envision?"

Naomi's spirits soared. Was he really buying this?

"As soon as you are ready to implement it, call a meeting of all your secretaries and directors and the Chief of the Joint Chiefs: the heads of every major cabinet body. Then you set this on the table and tell them they have 30 days in which to implement it and another 30 days in which to get all the required certificates signed and report back to you. We will gladly join you at this meeting, just to provide a little impetus, if any is required."

"How long do I have to think about this?" the President asked.

"About 15 minutes?" Serina replied. "You want to have time to schedule the cabinet meeting for tomorrow," Naomi added.

"I was thinking more in terms of a week or two," the President demurred.

"Totally unacceptable," Naomi said flatly. "We really need to have this implemented immediately."

"And if I don't agree?" the President was getting testy.

55

"It's really very simple, Mr. President," Naomi said quietly. "If you do not agree to our terms, we will begin negotiations with the Vice-President, when he succeeds you, tomorrow."

"Wait a minute," the President hedged, "you just said that you don't kill people."

"We don't, Mr. President," Serina stepped in. "But you could suddenly come down with a serious case of Helen Keller paralysis syndrome. There would be no choice but to replace you in office. You would still live a long healthy life."

They waited for that last comment to sink in.

"You can do that?" the President asked in total disbelief.

"In half a heartbeat," Naomi replied. "Want to test me?"

The President slowly shook his head.

"The ball is in your court now, Mr. President" Serina said. "You have offered no argument against our proposal. I assume that you consider it workable. As I said earlier, we are a peaceful people. I would very much like to see this affair end amicably and peacefully. What time shall we return tomorrow for the cabinet meeting?"

The President sighed. He could not, for a moment, believe that the entire might of the United States had just been brought to its knees by a couple of diminutive female aliens. Perhaps he could think of something else later, but for now, …

"I'll call the meeting for one o-clock tomorrow afternoon." The President said.

"I assume you will leave the appropriate passes for us?" Naomi asked. "We had a bit of a problem getting in to see you this morning."

"Of course!" The President assured them. "Now I really do need to get back to work."

Naomi and Serina thanked the President for his attention and assistance. Serina paused to scoop up their dresses on the way out of the Oval Office. They were both quite curious as to what the morrow would bring.

Chapter 7

Cabinet Meeting

It was rapidly approaching noon according to the grandfather clock standing against the wall. All was quiet in the cabinet meeting room at the White House. Naomi and Serina were lounging on the floor beneath the large mahogany table which filled the room.

No one had come in to set up refreshments on the sideboard. Perhaps it was too close to lunch.

No one had come to layout the documents to be discussed. Perhaps there were security issues.

Naomi was getting nervous. Perhaps something had gone wrong.

Serina noticed Naomi's case of nerves. Now she was getting nervous. "Can you reach the President from here?" she asked.

"Not quite, Naomi admitted. "He's a little too far away."

"How about his secretary?" Serina asked. "She's closer. Can you get her to take a look at his calendar?"

"Hmm, maybe." Naomi mused. "Let's see." Serina waited patiently. Then, in a few minutes, Naomi erupted. "This meeting isn't even on his calendar. That twit blew us off. I hesitate to think

58

what would have happened to us if we had tried to get into the White House this morning."

"Let's go pay him another visit," Serina suggested. She switched off the cameras as the two left the cabinet meting room and walked back into the secretary's office. Naomi made sure that no one could see them.

"According to his schedule," Naomi whispered, as she took a peek over the secretary's shoulder, he is talking to Senator Forbes right now. Let's take a look."

The two went to the door of the Oval Office, opened it and walked inside. Serina immediately switched her attention to the cameras in that office.

The Senator and the President were sitting on a couch. The President was reading a sheaf of papers. Naomi walked up behind the President and said, "Dear me, it looks like you forgot to call the cabinet meeting for one o'clock."

The President and the Senator both leaped to their feet and looked around for the source of the voice. The President recognized it, but the Senator was completely confused.

Serina joined the fun. She scooped up the papers that had fallen to the floor, handed them to the Senator and said, "Sorry to interrupt you, Senator, but the President is going to be a little busy for the next few hours. This way out." Still invisible, she grabbed his sleeve and directed the befuddled Senator to the door.

"Now, Mr. President," Naomi said, as she and Serina became visible, "it seems you may have forgotten about that cabinet meeting. I strongly suggest that you get to work."

"I have decided to put that off for a while. I didn't know how to get in touch with you … "

"You've got it all wrong, Mr. President," Naomi cut him off. "We are the ones who are calling the shots. You will have that cabinet meeting this afternoon and you will present and promote the directive we gave you without any significant changes. Otherwise," Naomi paused for effect, "the Vice-President will take over your duties and call the meeting tomorrow morning after he has been sworn in as President."

"It's your choice, Mr. President," Serina added, "but you have to decide now."

The President was in no mood to be told what to do in his own office. He turned and headed straight to his desk where he reached down to press the panic button. He was sure that with the Senator's testimony, he had a good case to get rid of these two whackos permanently. He never made it to the button.

Five minutes later, Naomi woke him up. He groaned, held his head in both hands and looked out at the two Elders with very bleary eyes. "What happened?" was the best he could manage.

"We just gave you a taste of what we have in store for you, if you don't shape up." Naomi said. "But next time we won't wake you up."

"You, you were all the way across the room." The President said in utter amazement. "You don't have a weapon. You really are aliens."

"I can't believe we had to put on a demonstration like this, just to get you to believe us?" Serina was so fed up with human nature!

"I'll call the cabinet meeting," The President said resignedly. "They will be here by two o'clock." He punched the intercom and gave the order to his secretary.

"We'll wait with you," Naomi said. "Just in case you get cold feet again. Besides, you will probably need some time to recover from your little episode."

While they were waiting, the President also found a properly cleared aide who could make copies of the Elders' directive.

At two o'clock the three left the Oval Office and walked down the hall to the cabinet room. Naomi and Serina opted to remain invisible for the moment. When they entered the room, they could see that the room was packed with people. There was barely room for the President to move down the table to his chair.

Naomi immediately whispered to the President, "Only the secretaries and directors and Chief of Staff." The President gave the order and over half the people left the room. In short order there was space to breathe.

The President distributed the document the Elders had devised. While the attendees were reading and digesting the document, Naomi and Serina, still invisible to everyone but the President, climbed up on the table and waited discreetly.

"Open for comment", the President said. There was immediately a barrage of questions and exclamations. The President just let the initial reactions settle down. Then he spoke.

"Ladies and gentlemen, I was in the same state of disbelief yesterday morning when two Elders walked into the White House, completely unmolested, and came into my office to present me with a copy of the document you have just read. I didn't believe it; it was just too improbable, too impossible. I have since become a believer.

"It is therefore my order that you take a copy of this document back to your respective department or agencies. You have just thirty days from today to reformat it according to your respective requirements, without, of course, changing any of the content, and disseminate it to all appropriate offices, considering the document's classification. You will then have an additional thirty days to implement the requirements of the document and get your confirmation sheets back through the chain of command to my office. Are there any questions?"

"Is this for real?" came from someone to the President's right.

"It is!" the President answered emphatically. "Are there any *intelligent* questions?"

"What do these 'Elders' look like?" Naomi was waiting for this question. She gave the President a gentle nudge. "See for yourself," he said.

At that moment, Naomi let all of the people at the table see her and Serina. There were several gasps, and even more mouths just hanging open. Someone at Serina's end of the table exclaimed, "They're naked!"

"As the document says," Naomi began, "we are a peaceful people. We do not rape or murder or mistreat anyone. All we want to do is simply go about our business without being molested. Recently, we had to rescue one of our number from the confines of a secret hospital room at Walter Reed, where she had been shackled to a bed for two days by someone from one of your agencies. Her only 'crime' was that she had *not* been hit by a bus. We will no longer tolerate even the chance of a repetition of such an injustice."

"And you expect this document to provide that?"

"Not initially," Naomi admitted. "It will take some time, and, I suspect, a few instances of 'Elder justice', before we will be truly safe. But it is a step in that direction. You will notice from the briefing that we are authorized to inflict 'Elder justice' when we deem it necessary. I believe that after we do that a few times, most humans will get the idea that it is far better to just live and let live."

"You said that you don't kill."

"We don't have to kill to make a point," Serina said. "There are a few things more terrible than death. Why don't you ask the President."

All eyes turned toward the President. "Yes, I can verify that," the President said rubbing his head, "There are indeed some things more terrifying than death. And, as far as I can tell, they don't leave a trace."

The room became quite sober. The President looked around the table. "Any more questions?" he asked. There were none. "Well, ladies and gentlemen," the President said, "I suggest that you get busy and start implementing that directive. I can assure you that I will be signing my Individual Certificate as soon as I get one. I expect to have all of your summary sheets on my desk within two months. In the meantime I recommend that you start behaving according to the requirements of that document. This meeting is adjourned."

After the attendees had filed out of the cabinet room on their way back to their respective offices, Serina and Naomi shook hands with the President, wished him well (Naomi actually did a little more than just *wish* him well) and headed back to the West Wing entrance.

"Boy, I am glad that we are finally headed home," Serina said.

"So am I," Naomi agreed. "Let's walk a bit. This weather is magnificent!."

Chapter 8

We're Being Followed

Naomi and Serina were feeling greatly elated. They had Just faced their greatest problem to date and had conquered it. They were like two kids who had spent their weekly allowance in the candy store and were now about to enjoy their sweets.

The weather was cooling as evening approached, but it was still clear and comfortable enough for Elders. There were many tourists still out and about taking in the sights.

Naomi and Serina crossed Pennsylvania Avenue and joined them in a stroll through Lafayette Square. They were not so much interested in the history or the statues as they were just being out in public with no threat from the authorities. They did attract an occasional stare from a tourist or two, but they were absolutely certain that they looked no worse, or more unusual than the rest of the tourists.

Scattered among the tourists were several politicians and businessmen going about their routine duties, scurrying between the various government buildings that abounded in the area. These were so intent on their business that they didn't have any time to gawk at the two little women wandering around the square.

"Let's take the Metro back home," Serina mused. "The Farragut West station is only a couple of blocks away."

"Sounds like a good idea," Naomi said. Then she added quietly, "First, let's take another trip around the square. I think we're being followed."

Serina reached out, but could not detect anything unusual. "What gives you that idea?" she whispered.

"I keep getting the same two vibes," Naomi answered. "They aren't looking at the statues and they aren't on business. No, let me change that. They are looking at the statues, but they are not thinking about the statues."

"Okay," Serina agreed, "that is weird. Where are they, now?"

"Over by Jackson's statue," Naomi nodded slightly in the direction from which they had just come.

"Why don't we just go over and have it out with them?" Serina was ready for a fight.

"Not here, not now," Naomi cautioned. "They are doing their best to stay 180° away from us at all times. If we approached them, they would just move off. Besides, I want to know who sent them. Odds are that it was someone who was in that cabinet meeting and ought to know better."

"Well, we can't go home with them around," Serina stated the obvious. "How do we shake them?"

"How well do you remember this area of Washington?" Naomi asked. She was looking nonchalantly toward the north, using her eyes more than her head to direct her gaze.

"What do you want to know?" Serina asked in return.

"Is there a bus stop at the corner of I Street and Connecticut?" Naomi was again looking at the statue in front of them.

Serina gave the question some thought. She had not been in downtown Washington that often. But she had a good retention for detail. "Yes, there is." She answered.

"Okay," Naomi whispered, pointing out some imaginary detail on the statue. "Keep that goal in mind and follow my lead. Also keep alert to any potential danger. If anything threatens, don't depend on me, cancel the threat yourself."

With that, Naomi turned right and headed slowly toward the north exit from the square. Serina followed closely on her heels. She was trying desperately not to look like an Oriental wife dutifully following her husband. She quickly caught up to Naomi and continued walking beside her.

Naomi was paying close attention to the pair who were tailing them. They had suddenly forgotten their interest in the Jackson statue and were also heading toward the north exit.

Once on the sidewalk of H Street, Naomi and Serina proceeded to cross the street. Once across the street, Naomi stopped and signaled Serina to switch the traffic light. As soon as the crossing light had switched off and traffic was blocking their pursuers, Naomi made a great show of giving Serina a hug, whispering to her to take it slowly, and kissing her good-bye. Then Naomi turned and headed north on 16th Street.

Serina was momentarily stunned as she watched Naomi move away from her. Then the plan dawned on her: the two people following them would be forced to split up. One would follow Naomi and the other would be forced to follow her. She immediately turned and proceeded west on H Street toward Connecticut at a leisurely stroll.

Naomi walked slowly until she was certain that only one person was following. Then she gradually sped up to a rapid walk toward I Street. If Naomi's plan was going to work, she had to get to the bus stop first.

As she walked, Naomi did her best to monitor the man who was following her. Every so often he seemed to be momentarily distracted. Naomi pondered the situation. When Naomi got to the next corner, she crossed I Street at the last minute before the light changed, again leaving her pursuer waiting.

Naomi turned left and made her way toward the bus stop at the end of the block. There was no bus in sight, but Naomi had no intention of taking a bus. She quickly moved through a small crowd of people outside the Brown Bag Restaurant and ducked into a doorway. She waited. In less than a minute, her pursuer passed by the doorway.

"I'm over here," Naomi said. The man stopped and turned toward her. For the moment he was speechless. Naomi had seen to that.

Chapter 9

The Bus Stop

Naomi led the man over to the bench at the bus stop. The bench was vacant. It was late in the afternoon, but not yet quitting time.

"Let's sit down," Naomi suggested. The man complied.

"Now, suppose you give me your gun and ID and phone," Naomi said. She backed up her request with a little mental prodding and the man complied. The gun she emptied and put back in his holster. The ID provided his name, James Walker, and his organization, Homeland Security.

"Well, James," Naomi said. "Let's just relax for a few minutes until your friend gets here."

Sure enough, in a few minutes, Serina appeared across the street. She took in what had transpired at the bus stop and quickly turned the corner and waited. As soon as her pursuer arrived at the corner, Serina distracted him momentarily until Naomi was able to take control of his mind.

At that point, Serina was able to walk him across the street to the bench. He was encouraged to sit and was duly divested of his gun and ID.

Serina took a seat on the bench as Naomi emptied the agent's gun and replaced it in his holster.

They looked briefly at the ID. It had also been issued by Homeland Security.

"I assume you have a car somewhere in the vicinity," Naomi said to the two agents. Neither made any indication. "Look," she said more sternly, "You weren't conceived out here on the street by miraculous conception. You came by car. Now you can either tell me where the car is, or I'm going to start playing games with your anatomy."

The two men remained stoic.

"Okay," Naomi said, somewhat exasperated, "I know you can't talk. Just nod if you want to cooperate." There were no nods.

"Alright, you asked for it," Naomi said. "You want to be big brave heroes. This is what a serious case of gout feels like."

The two men winced in agony.

"I know," Serina said sympathetically. "It hurts. But just think how much more it will hurt if we move it up your leg to your calf. How about a Charley Horse, and you unable to move your leg to relax the muscle."

Naomi followed Serina's suggestion and the two men were almost unable to handle the strong, persisting pain.

In fact, the 'pain' the two men were experiencing was not in their toes or calves; it was just in their minds. Their legs had not been harmed in the least. But they did not know that. All they knew was that it hurt terribly and they were unable to do anything to ease the pain. They could not even scream.

There were two men sitting in a black sedan parked at the other end of the block on I Street. They had been watching everything that was happening at the bus stop. To them it appeared that the other two agents had met with the two targets of their investigation and were having a conversation with them on the bench at the bus stop. They had seen nothing to indicate otherwise and were waiting for further orders.

Back on the bench, Serina and Naomi were about to panic. It was too close to quitting time to wait any longer. In a few minutes the area would be swarming with people on the way home – theirs or someone else's. The busses would be running in rapid succession to clear the people out. The Metro would be crowded!

"Last chance!" Naomi told the two agents. "Next stop is your balls. Call the car or you will never want to have sex again."

The two agents remained stoic. Naomi wanted to admire their dedication and courage, but she didn't have the time. She unleashed a massive amount of pain between their legs. James gave in. He wiggled his head dramatically to indicate he was ready to capitulate.

Naomi lessened his pain and allowed him to speak. "What is their number?" she asked.

"2225551212" James whispered. Serina entered the number into the phone and pressed connect. A man's voice came on the line, "Yes?" Naomi held the phone to James mouth. "No tricks!" she whispered in his ear. Just tell them to drive up to the bus stop.

"Drive up to the bus stop," James said weakly into the phone. Serina broke the connection.

Serina and Naomi searched the street for a car that had suddenly begun to move. They saw a black sedan that had been parked about a block away coming toward them. As the car pulled into the bus stop, Serina severed all communications and killed the engine. Naomi froze the occupants in place.

It was a simple matter to remove the occupants' ID and render their weapons useless. These ID's also came from Homeland Security.

"Alright, James," Naomi said, "We know you all came from Homeland Security. Now we need to know who told you to follow us. You know what it has felt like to try to oppose us. You haven't felt anything yet compared to what you are going to feel unless you answer this last question. Just tell us what we want to know and we'll leave you in peace. You have one chance. Talk to me." Naomi released James speech function and waited.

The agent looked at his partner seated beside him in an absolute stupor. He saw the two agents in the car, completely immobile. He thought about the pain he had felt. His assailants had not lifted a finger against him. He did not doubt their ability to do just what they had threatened. He had a wife waiting for him at home. He decided that further resistance would eventually be futile.

"We were part of the Director's body guard. He gave us our instructions when he left a cabinet meeting at the White House."

"Bingo!" thought Naomi. That is the only way they could have been on the scene so quickly.

"People are beginning to look at us," Serina cautioned. "It's quitting time."

Naomi quickly put all of the agents to sleep and erased any memory of what happened from their minds. The Two Elders got up from the bench and headed west to the Metro station, now only a block away. They would have loved to be around when the four agents were found, but in this case, discretion was far better than curiosity. They had some planning to do before they tackled the source of their problem.

Chapter 10

Homeland Security

When the alarm went off, the first thing Charlie Weber did was to check the weather. He couldn't tell you why, if you asked him. He worked indoors. A climate-controlled car would pick him up in ninety minutes and take him to his place of employment.

In the summer he would go out to his pool now for an early morning swim. But it was October, an exceptionally warm October, but not suitable for outdoor swimming. Therefore, Charlie went for a short jog through his Palisades neighborhood before he showered and ate breakfast.

Promptly at nine o'clock, a car pulled up outside his front door. Charlie, now decked out in his customary dark suit and red tie left his house and climbed into the backseat though the door held open by his chauffer.

The chauffer resumed his position behind the wheel and they were off into traffic. They were closely followed by a car containing four armed men. Charlie Weber was the Director of Homeland Security and he never went anywhere in Washington without a body guard.

As soon as they were moving, Charlie picked up a car phone and called his secretary. It was his custom to confirm his morning appointments before he arrived at his office.

A few miles to the south, breakfast was also over for Naomi and Serina and they were preparing for their visit to Homeland Security.

"Same dresses as yesterday?" Serina asked.

"Why not," Naomi answered. "We don't sweat and we didn't spill anything on them or roll around in the dirt." Then she added, "Since this is our first 'assassination', I think I will touch base with the Council."

Serina didn't answer, so Naomi took that as agreement and went over to the computer. She called up the Kaleidoscope and sent off a query for a consult with the Council. In less than fifteen minutes, the Chief of the Council was on the line. Naomi filled her in on the happenings of the day before. When she finished with the tale of the interrogation of the Homeland Security agents, she told the Chief that she and Serina were off to chastise the Secretary for his violation of the directive he had just been told to implement. Her response was brief, "Concur" was all she said.

"Here," Serina announced as she tossed a dress to Naomi. "Shall I call for a limo?"

"Might as well." Naomi agreed. "This is going to be harder than the White House was. I think it is actually better guarded and the Secretary will be expecting us."

By this time, Charlie Weber had been dropped outside the DHS headquarters building and had found his way to his office. On the way in he stopped by his secretary's desk to inquire if there was anything new on his docket for the day. She reported that the day was still clear.

The Secretary went into his office, draped his suit coat over the back of his chair and sat down at his desk to look over the reports that had arrived overnight.

As he shuffled through them, he scowled and reached for the intercom. He pushed the button marked CoS. "Martin", he said in a loud, demanding voice, "where are the reports from the four agents I sent on the special mission yesterday?"

"I'll be right there," Martin answered. In a moment he was in the Secretary's office standing, empty handed, in front of the Secretary's desk.

"I'm terribly sorry, sir," Martin said, "but there are no reports from James and company."

"Why not?" the Secretary growled. He was suddenly not in a good mood.

"There is a report from the Metro Police on your desk," Martin explained. "About six PM yesterday, they were called to a bus stop at 16th and I Street where a government vehicle was blocking the bus stop. The Police say they found an unoccupied vehicle which had been somehow disabled. They ordered that the vehicle be impounded. Then they discovered four men sitting on the bench at the bus stop. The men did not appear to be injured, but they were totally non-responsive. The Police report says they appeared to be intoxicated or under the influence of some drug. They each had an unloaded weapon, but no identification. They were first transported to the District jail for booking, then to a local hospital for observation. I believe these men were James and the others you sent on that surveillance mission yesterday. I have sent a couple of other agents over to the hospital to verify that. They will also check the car at the impound lot to see if it is ours."

Martin had been speaking non-stop. He now paused for a breath.

"That is the most remarkable bunch of drivel I have ever heard," the Secretary exploded. Then, after a moment's reflection, he continued in a calmer voice, "but not totally unbelievable. Follow up on this and keep me posted. Let me know if you hear anything from James."

Martin acknowledged the order and beat a hasty retreat from the Secretary's office.

The town car picked up Naomi and Serina at Volta Park and whisked them out to Nebraska St NW near the American University. The driver pulled up to the guard post and announced that his passengers had a ten o'clock appointment with the Secretary. After the usual list checking and prompting, the guard waved them into the compound and directed them to the headquarters building.

The Headquarters Building had a red brick façade and was some three stories tall. It effectively hid a large complex of connected buildings behind it. Naomi and Serina left the town car and went in the main entrance. At the next guard station, they secured the appropriate passes and were escorted by a guard to the Secretary's outer office. Serina noted several surveillance systems scattered about. None appeared to be super sophisticated, but, for the moment, she left them alone.

A woman in the outer office, presumably the secretary, was easily convinced that Serina and Naomi were indeed just in time for their scheduled appointment. The guard was satisfied and left them to her care. The woman was about to announce their arrival when Naomi stopped her. She and Serina simply walked to the door of the Secretary's office, opened it slightly and edged inside.

Serina immediately located and scrambled the surveillance cameras. Naomi made sure that the Secretary was alone and that he could not see them. The two then doffed the dresses they had been wearing and walked over to the Secretary's desk. He was sitting there concentrating heavily on a document in front of him.

Naomi saw his copy of the executive order sitting on one side of his desk. She picked it up and slid it on top of the document he was reading. The Secretary startled and looked up. At that point, she let him see her and Serina.

Naomi had expected more of a reaction, but the Secretary just squinted his eyes and scowled at them with his lips in a thin straight line. "What did you do to my agents?" he spat out.

"I simply put them to sleep for a little while," Naomi chuckled. "They had done nothing wrong; we just had to get them out of our way. They will wake up in a day or so and be perfectly alright. When they do wake up, they won't remember anything of their adventure."

"You on the other hand," Serina began, "are another case entirely."

"Yes," Naomi added sternly, "you were completely aware of the President's order to leave us alone and you deliberately violated it by sending those men after us. You must realize we had absolutely no idea what their actual orders were. We only knew that they were tracking us for some nefarious purpose."

"You are out of your minds!" the Secretary protested. "They were just performing normal surveillance of the area around the White House. Your presence there was entirely accidental."

"That is the sorriest excuse I have ever heard," Serina scolded. Every move they made indicated that they were intentionally following us."

"And, when we finally stopped them," Naomi continues, "they freely and clearly admitted that you had ordered them to follow us. Well, maybe not freely, but clearly."

"Now," Serina, said, pointing to the executive directive, "I call your attention to paragraph 4 of the briefing sheet."

The Secretary looked at the paragraph Serina had indicated. He suddenly had a very bad feeling. So bad, in fact, that he quickly reached under his desk and pressed his panic button.

Naomi and Serina could hear running feet approaching the Secretary's office. Both office doors burst open and several armed men rushed into the office. The guards came to a screeching stop in the middle of the office, stood back-to-back and looked around for the cause of the problem. They could see nothing.

"What's the problem, Sir?" sergeant of the guard finally asked. He was looking quite confused.

The Secretary had not yet realized in all the confusion that Naomi and Serina had disappeared. He looked where they had been standing, and, seeing nothing, started searching the office for any sign of them. "They were right here," he stammered. "Two of them."

"Two people?" the sergeant questioned. He motioned the other guards to start searching the office. The quickly spread out looking in every corner, behind the furniture, under the furniture, behind the drapes. They found nothing.

"I am sorry, sir," the sergeant reported. "We saw no one leave as we approached your office and there is no one here."

"Perhaps they managed to escape, somehow," the Secretary reluctantly admitted. "Make one more thorough physical sweep, just to be sure."

The guards again moved through the office, searching around the larger furniture, moving the smaller pieces. Looking behind and under and over. One guard even approached the Secretary's desk with the thought of sweeping his arm over the top of it. On seeing the expression on the Secretary's face, he thought better of it.

In the end, the sergeant of the guard reported finding nothing and took his leave of the Secretary.

Secretary Weber collapsed back into his chair.

"Well, that was certainly exciting!" Naomi exclaimed as she and Serina jumped down from the top of the Secretary's desk. "But let's not do that again. Oh, by the way, Serina has disabled your panic buttons, both of them."

"Now if you would be so good, Mr. Secretary," Serina asked, "please call your deputy and ask him to come into your office."

The Secretary looked somewhat confused, but did as he was asked. In a few minutes, the Deputy Secretary of Homeland Security, Mr. Alan Burke, came into the office.

Naomi picked up the executive directive from the Secretary's desk and handed it to Mr. Burke.

"This directive," Naomi began, "was issued by the President yesterday afternoon at the cabinet meeting. Your boss was present at the meeting where the directive was explained and any questions answered. The President ordered that the directive be implemented within 30 days and a complete briefing cycle be completed within 60 days.

"My companion and were present at the meeting. After the meeting we decided to take a stroll through Lafayette Park. During that stroll we discovered we were being followed by two men. We managed to isolate the men and disarm them.

"Then we discovered that they were being backed up by two more men in a vehicle. We were able to isolate them and disarm them as well. We discussed the matter with these men and one of them admitted that they had all been assigned to follow and observe us by the Secretary of Homeland Security. We left those men sitting on a bench at a bus stop with their disabled vehicle. I am sure you have, by now, heard of this incident.

"We have come here this morning to discuss the issue with the Secretary. He has been unable to persuade us that he did not issue that order following the cabinet meeting at which he was explicitly told, by the President, not to do just such a thing."

"We have been authorized," Serina said, "by our Council, to take punitive action in accordance with paragraph four of the Briefing Sheet."

Mr. Burke quickly looked through the sheets he was holding until he had noted the cited paragraph. "And just how does this involve me?" he asked.

"You will be the witness to our punishment," Naomi said. "You may explain what happens next in any manner you choose, just so long as you do not disclose the information in the directive to unauthorized personnel. In such a case, we would have to come back for you."

The Secretary was rapidly becoming apoplectic. He realized that he was staring death, or the equivalent thereof, in the face. He knew he had to make a break for it. He got two steps before Naomi stopped him in mid stride. He stood for a moment and then slowly crumpled to the floor.

Mr. Burke stood in awe of what he had seen. Naomi and Serina had just stood there. Neither had moved a muscle; but his boss was now lying on the floor – dead.

"He is not dead," Naomi explained. "If you check, you will find that he is still breathing, and will continue to do so for years. He is simply blind, deaf, mute, and partially paralyzed. Oh, and there is nothing your medical science can do to remedy the situation. I recommend they do not try."

"Our job is done," Serina said. "We will be leaving now. Please do not attempt to duplicate your predecessor's mistakes. Your President ordered you to leave us alone. I strongly suggest that you follow his order."

Naomi and Serina retrieved their dresses and left the Secretary's office, ever vigilant for an impending attack. They did not hear an alarm. There were no guards rushing about brandishing their weapons. At the entrance, they asked the guard to summon their vehicle. When it arrived at the door, they got in and left Homeland Security.

Chapter 11

Cheese It! The Fuzz!

When Naomi and Serina returned home they sent a message to the Council telling them that they had attended to the problem. Elena responded and congratulated the two on a speedy resolution to the problem. She also asked if there were likely to be any repercussions.

"We'll be watching, just in case," Naomi responded. "But I don't think so. I had the Deputy Secretary watch the demise of his boss. I think he got the message."

"So we're safe now," Serina mused. "You want to go out walking tomorrow and test your theory?"

"Not unless it's absolutely necessary," Naomi was quick to respond. "Remember, it will take two months to fully implement the directive. Unless, of course, the government's up to its usual efficiency. Then it may take awhile longer. But at least we're on our way. That is a step forward,"

"Here's your supper!" Serina teased as she threw a piece of cheese to Naomi.

Just as Naomi and Serina were settling down for a nice quiet evening at home, the telephone began buzzing so loudly that it almost walked itself off the table.

Naomi jumped up and grabbed it just as it teetered on the edge. She looked at the caller id. The call was from Ali. That was decidedly different. She and Serina had called Ali often enough to arrange transportation, but he had never called them before.

"Ali", Naomi informed Serina, who stared back in disbelief. Naomi considered the matter briefly, then she just shrugged and answered the call. She also turned on the speaker, so Serina could listen in.

"Hello, Ali," Naomi said, " trying to drum up some business?"

"Sorry if I disturbed you," Ali said. "No, I am not trying to drum up business – though I do enjoy our trips together.

"Listen! When I'm trolling for customers, I sometimes turn on the police radio – just for news on road closures, you understand."

"Sure, I understand," Naomi shot back.

"Tonight," Ali continued, "I heard something disturbing." Ali paused, as though trying to figure out where to go next.

"I'm sorry you heard something disturbing," Naomi offered. "Is there anything I can do to help?"

"That's just it," Ali said. "You appear to be the problem."

"What problem?" Naomi asked. "Ali start making sense!"

"It was the police call," Ali said. "I think it was all about you."

"That's good, Ali," Naomi encouraged. "Now, what did the police call say?"

"It was a BOLO," Ali reported.

"What's a 'bolo'?" Naomi asked. At this question, Serina, who had been chuckling quietly at the previous conversation, suddenly perked up her ears.

"A BOLO is police slang for 'Be On the Look Out'," Ali explained. "And you two are the subject of this latest one. At least I think you are."

"Just what did the police report say?" Naomi asked.

"It was a BOLO for two women, about four and one-half feet tall, plain white skin, black eyes, sparse hair, possibly covered by a wig, wearing pastel dresses and sandals," Ali recited. "It said they were wanted as persons of interest and advised all personnel to take them into custody if they were seen."

"Ali, are you sure this isn't some sort of mistake?" At this point Naomi was becoming somewhat concerned.

"I swear … " Ali started, then he added, "Got a fare! Bye, now" And the line went dead.

"Now, what do we do?" Serina asked as Naomi put the phone back in the center of the table.

"Better question," Naomi said, "How do we explain it? What did we do to attract the attention of the police?"

"Well," Serina recited. "This morning we sort of disabled the Secretary for Homeland Security. Do you think that Burke character would have called in the police?"

"No," Naomi replied. "He didn't impress me as a weakling who would rely on some other agency to do what he should be doing."

"Hmm!?" Serina mused.

Naomi looked incredulously at Serina. "Don't you think we convinced him to lay off?"

"Actually," Serina admitted, "I didn't really like the way he was looking at us. If he had decided discretion was the best way to go, he would have pulled in his horns. But if he were also still pissed over what we had done to his boss, he might just have had the brilliant idea to use a non-federal agency to do his dirty work for him."

"That's a great idea," Naomi agreed, much to Serina's pleasure, "but I am afraid it won't fly in this case."

"Why not?" Serina asked impetuously.

"Because, my Dear," Naomi explained, "you chose white dresses for us to wear today instead of the pastels we wore when we visited the White House."

Serina stopped to think for a moment, then she nodded in resignation. "But all we did there was support the President while he imposed the directive on his staff. Nothing in that should require police intervention."

"What about the action we took afterwards?" Naomi suggested. "I seem to recall that we left a Homeland Security vehicle blocking a downtown bus stop. And a few rather pickled agents taking up space on a public bench. It is highly likely that the police intervened in that mess before the DHS managed to take control."

"Bingo!" Serina announced. "If the police were called to clear the bus stop and found the agents, they would have interrogated any witnesses who might have seen what happened. If the police ever did get back to DHS, I'm sure that Burke would not have dissuaded them from pursuing an arrest."

"That's pretty much it," Naomi confirmed. "Now what?"

"Well, we're fairly safe as long as we stay indoors," Serina suggested. "They don't know where we live or they would already have been knocking in our door. Oh, by the way, that cheese we had for supper was the last of our stash."

"Great!" Naomi summarized, "We can either stay indoors and slowly starve to death or we can go out to get groceries and run the risk of being picked up by the police."

"If we go out," Serina suggested, "we could always wear pants and long sleeve shirts and hats."

"Somehow, I just don't think that is the solution," Naomi said. "Why don't we sleep on this and figure out something better tomorrow?"

"Yeah," Serina concurred. "Perhaps Ali will call us and tell us the BOLO has been rescinded."

"In your dreams, maybe," Naomi muttered as she headed for the bedroom.

Chapter 12

You Said This Would Be Easy

The situation had not improved any the next morning. Serina pointed out that the police still had not broken down their door, but that didn't help much. There was some leftover milk, only slightly sour, that Naomi found hiding out in the back of the fridge. She served that for breakfast. It was not starting out as a good day.

"Okay," Serina said at last, "we've got to resolve this police issue. As I recall, you said that dealing with local police departments would be easy. What do you recommend we do?"

"Hey," Naomi said in her defense, "I wasn't thinking about a large metro PD when I made that statement. They mat not be as potentially deadly as the Feds, but they aren't Podunk PD, either."

"I'll give you a pass on that," Serina granted. "But we have to handle this issue before it gets worse."

"Alright, let's look at the situation," Naomi suggested. "If we are just 'persons of interest' that means they haven't decided to level real charges against us. Perhaps they are considering simultaneous mental breakdowns or something."

"In a pig's eye!" Serina offered her opinion.

"No, really," Naomi protested. "We need to find out what the police know, or think they know, before we plunge into this much further. We need to talk to the Chief of Police."

"Well, we talked to the President; this should be easy." Serina immediately clasped her hand over her mouth as soon as she realized what she had just said.

Naomi properly pointed out that, compared to the White House, the Metro Police building was like a fortress. Neither of the two relished a major onslaught into a fortress. Besides, Naomi admitted, she really didn't want to leave any more humans crumpled on the ground without a functioning brain. It just wasn't decent – unless there was no other choice.

"What choice do we have?" Serina asked. "I don't think calling the Chief up on the phone is going to work."

"How about a face-to-face meeting outside the PD for starters?" Naomi asked in return. "Somewhere so public that we'll both feel safe."

"The bus stop was really public, and look what happened there," Serina was right on topic. "Can we compromise on inside public?"

Naomi went into deep thought mode. Suddenly she perked up. "That McDonalds' by the Mall has at least three exits, maybe four. What could be safer than McDonalds?"

Serina had a different idea. "As I recall," she said, "a young woman was badly beaten just for using the restroom in a McDonalds. How about the Enid Haupt Garden on Independence? That is out in the open, but it is protected by a wall, has an back entrance onto the Mall and has two Metro stations within easy running distance."

Naomi agreed. Then there was the matter of how to contact the Chief. That was easy – a phone call. Serina turned on the computer and looked up the best number. Naomi made a call to Ali.

Ali showed up at the local grocery store in twenty minutes. Naomi and Serina, wearing long coats over their pastel dresses, sandals and curly wigs, quickly jumped into his back seat. "Okay, Ali," Naomi explained, "here's the deal. Just drive like a snake: no circles, no long straight lines, no repeats, cover the town. We need to make a phone call and we don't want to be traced. Got it?" Ali nodded and took off.

Naomi dialed the number for the Metro PD on her cell phone and asked to speak with the Chief. She got a secretary. She again asked to speak with the Chief. "On what subject?" the voice asked.

"I am one of the women of interest who was wearing a pastel dress," Naomi said. "More than a minute delay and I will hang up." She waited and started counting off seconds. Forty seconds later another female voice came on the line.

"Hello, I am Laura Springer, Chief of Police, what can I do for you?"

"I would like to meet with you, face-to-face," Naomi said, "answer your questions and get this

BOLO rescinded. If you agree, I'll continue this conversation." Naomi paused.

After a few seconds, the Chief said, "I agree. Where shall we meet?"

"In the Enid A. Haupt Gardens on Independence in sixty minutes. Come alone. No cars, no backup, no air cover. If you follow these directions, I promise to answer all your questions to the best of my ability. I also guarantee you will not be harmed in any way; and will be free to leave at any time."

"Yes, but ... " the Chief tried to discuss the options.

"No 'buts'," Naomi said. "This phone can not be traced or tracked. This conversation is over."

"Okay, Ali,", Naomi told their driver, take us to the Smithsonian Metro station. Direct route."

Naomi slipped Ali his usual fee when she and Serina emerged from the taxi at the Metro station. The two then made their way carefully down the street to the Haupt gardens. The lunch crowd had dissipated. The weather was cloudy and very cool. It was not conducive to tourists. The sidewalks were relatively clear. Both of the Elders kept a keen watch out for any sign of a police vehicle.

Serina had been quietly monitoring the time. "Twenty minutes to go," she announced. "What are we going to do now?"

Naomi had been checking out the gardens. Most of the little trees were losing their leaves, but the two large ones were still in full leaf. "Let's go climb a tree," She suggested. In a few minutes the two were up the tree, well hidden within the branches, and with an excellent view of the entry way.

Serina kept a watch for gadgets and Naomi prepared to take control of any dangerous humans. The remaining twenty minutes passed – slowly. Naomi was beginning to feel like they had been stood up. Then a brightly colored Metro Police car pulled up at the entrance. The back door opened and a woman stepped out. She turned and headed for the entrance to the gardens. The car remained, its lights flashing.

Naomi sent the presumed Chief a subtle hint. Just before she entered the gardens she turned and spoke to the driver of the car. It left the area and turned north at the corner of the block.

Naomi and Serina silently dropped from the tree and followed the Chief into the garden. Once she entered, she looked around undecided as to how to next proceed.

"We're right here," Naomi said. The startled woman spun around and stared at the two. She did not immediately reach for a weapon. Serina immediately disabled the woman's camera and radio. "May I see a photo ID?" Naomi asked. The woman pulled a wallet out of her small black shoulder bag and proffered a driver's license. It identified her as Laura Springer and the picture matched. "Police ID?" Naomi persisted. Again the woman reached into her purse and produced her Police ID and badge. The name and photo matched.

"Thank you," Naomi said. "Now, you should know that we mean you no harm and you are free to leave any time you wish. But please realize this. If, at any time while we are talking, we feel any threat, be it a vehicle, a weapon or a person, you will not leave this place with any free will or mental ability left."

That caused Laura's eyes to open a bit. She looked around for the source of a threat. Then she recognized her error and turned her full attention on Naomi and Serina.

"My name is Naomi," Naomi said, "and this is my companion, Serina. We do not use last names. We live in the District. We understand that you issued a BOLO for us. We have no desire to be hassled or arrested by the police, as we have committed no crime. We are asking you to rescind that BOLO and leave us in peace. If you have any questions, we will be happy to answer them – in so far as we can."

"Well, for starters," Laura began, "You have threatened my well being. And from reports I have received, you participated in the incapacitation of four federal agents. Why should I not consider you criminals?"

"Good question," Serina responded. "The federal agents we dealt with were armed and had been deliberately sent to harass us, and possibly do even more, by a person who had just been directed by the President of the United States to do no such thing. When faced with four strong men who were armed and capable of shooting us, we had reason to fear for our lives. You will note, if you follow the incident, that we did them no permanent physical harm. We simply disarmed them, rendered their weapons useless and left them incapable of following us or harassing us further."

"By now," Naomi added, "They probably have fully recovered from their encounter with us. In point of fact, their boss, the person who disobeyed a direct order from the President, will never recover from his meeting with us."

"We did not kill him," Serina hastened to add. "We simply left him deaf, dumb, blind and paralyzed. He will never be able to threaten us again."

"You speak of actions by the President," Laura said, "how do you know about these actions?"

"We prepared the instructions and were with the President when he gave the instructions to members of his cabinet," Naomi said.

"Why did the President issue these orders?" Laura wanted the big picture; she wasn't going to get it.

"We have certain qualities that may some day be of invaluable use to this country," Serina responded. "More than that we can not say. I strongly encourage you not to inquire further. Should you ask a member of the President's cabinet and they answer you, they will have placed both their and your continued viability in severe jeopardy."

"We are not the only ones of our kind in Washington," Naomi explained. "Should your BOLO ensnare some of the others, they would have no idea why they were being hassled and could react instantly out of fear."

"As a matter of conjecture, "Serina added, "it was quite probably your well-meant involvement in a simple bus accident a week or so back, that caused the Federal Government to begin harassing us in the first place."

"And you're asking me to just take all of this on faith?" Laura asked.

"No," Naomi pointed out. "You have seen what we can do. There is no 'faith' in that. It is real."

"And I just cancel the BOLO?"

Neither of the Elders could read the Chief's intent, so they both said, "Yes!" in unison.

"We do no harm to anyone – without provocation. We just want to live our lives in peace, and without police intervention." Serina said.

"Okay, I'll cancel the BOLO," the Chief said, "until you start leaving some more unexplained bodies lying around on street corners. Then you can continue this conversation in jail."

"That looks like a handcuff case on your belt," Serina said. "If it isn't just for your makeup, put the cuffs on me."

Laura looked askance at the two standing before her. Naomi nodded her head, "Go ahead," she said.

The chief took out a pair of handcuffs. Serina held out her hands, and Laura fastened the handcuffs snugly about her wrists.

"Are you sure they are secure?" Serina asked.

Laura tested the cuffs and nodded. As soon as Laura let go of the cuffs, they clicked open and fell to the ground. Serina promptly picked up the cuffs and handed them back to Laura. "You need a better grade cuff," Serina said.

"The same thing would happen if you put us in jail," Naomi Said. "Only then we would be irritated and might not only disable a few guards, but also pay you a little visit on our way home."

"Okay, I get the point," Laura said. "Can I call my car, now?"

Naomi nodded. Then she added, "We will leave the area after you have gone. Remember the Homeland Security issue – do not have anyone try to follow us, on the ground or in the air – drones included."

The Chief nodded in agreement. Serina cleared the Chief's radio and the Chief called her driver. The car pulled up outside the garden in a matter of seconds and she departed. Naomi and Serina waited for a few minutes, then they checked the surrounding area for surveillance. Finding none, they walked over to the Metro and rode home.

Chapter 13

Just Another Day

When Naomi and Serina got back to their neighborhood, they stopped at the neighborhood market long enough to get some food for the morrow. Back at their apartment, Naomi carried her bag into the kitchen and started to put the groceries away. Serina set her bag on the table, accidentally kicking their cell phone across the carpet in the process.

She picked up the phone and noticed that there was a voice mail message from Ali. This was suddenly getting too common for her liking. She switched the sound on and called to Naomi, who was still putting the groceries away.

"Just heard another police call canceling the BOLO," Ali said. "Presume you had something to do with that. Congratulations! Ooops, got a fare. Bye now."

"Well," Naomi said, "it looks like we did win another round. I wonder how many more we'll have to fight."

Serina cleared the message and went to help Naomi with the groceries.

Later that evening, while Naomi and Serina were sitting around digesting supper, the latter broached a topic that had been bothering her.

"Naomi, we've spent a lot of time this week trying to 'convince' various people to leave us alone. How much longer? How many more agencies, departments and VIP's are we going to have to 'convince'?"

"Whoa," Naomi replied, "Don't burn out on me so soon. Remember, this is our job. We were sent here to help protect the Elder community from any possible adverse action."

"Yes, I know," Serina said. "And I completely support that mission. But, rescuing Divina is more my idea of protecting the community. I'm not so sure I really like what we have been doing since."

"Look at it this way," Naomi countered. "What we did this week will protect a thousand Divina's, not just here in Washington, but all over the country. If we hadn't done that we would be running around all over the place rescuing them from goodness knows what.

"And that's important, now that we know about Divina. I still can't get over her news. Ever since 2010 we have had women out there somewhere who can give birth to Elder children. Not only that, but it looks like their Elder children will also give birth to other Elders. We have some twenty years of new Elders out there, with no end in sight.

"Just think what might happen if the humans ever got wind of that."

"Yeah," Serina agreed, "I see what you mean. I once had a chance to chat with Red Hawk and she told me of the problems the Elder community had with human discrimination. If they ever did get wind of the fact that Elders could one day out breed them, we all could be in big trouble.

"But even if we do convince them now to leave us alone, what is to keep them from just abrogating these agreements in the future, as if they never happened?"

"That's what we are here to prevent," Naomi answered. "We've got a breather right now. But we have no idea what may happen in the future.

"It's true that we have the Federal Government sewn up, and, if we can lick the Washington PD, we can lick almost any police agency."

"That's just my point," Serina sighed. "Sure, we can beat them, but we're just two little Elders in one town. How about all the other Elders, the new mutants, who will be popping out all over the country? Will they be able to protect themselves? The mutants won't know anything about us. They won't even understand what is happening to them when they hit puberty. This is a disaster just looking for somewhere to happen."

"Good question," Naomi said, pausing to consider the problem. "The children from the original mothers have now made it to child bearing age. Not only the 'human' children we left behind, but the other children they may have had and the children their children have had. It's absolutely mind boggling!"

"And they *will* be scattered all over the country," Serina added, "even foreign countries by now. You know," she mused, "at this rate, we may eventually out breed the humans."

"That'll take a lot of centuries," Naomi pointed out, "but, technically, I suppose it is possible.

"Well, if I have a vote," Serina said, "how about an assignment in Europe? Now that would be exciting!"

"Dream on," Naomi chided.

"Speaking of dreaming," Serina announced. "I'm going to hit the mattress.

As Serina walked back to the bedroom, the Kaleidoscope suddenly beeped, indicating an incoming call. Naomi walked over to the desk and acknowledged the call.

The call was from Mara, the Sentinel in Atlanta. She had just run into her first mutant and had contacted the Council for guidance. Their only guidance was to contact Naomi and Serina in Washington. Naomi asked Mara for a synopsis of her problem.

She reported that a mutant had been detained by the FBI with the aid of the Atlanta PD. The mutant was being held incommunicado and Mara said the she did not have the resources to get close to her.

Naomi suggested that a new directive on Elder harassment was being disseminated now and Mara should have the FBI immediately contact the Attorney General for guidance on this action.

As for the Atlanta PD, Naomi suggested that Mara isolate a few officers of the Atlanta PD in a public place and leave them with a two day case of Helen-Keller Syndrome. When they have recovered contact the Chief of Police and have a heart-to-heart talk with him/her about not harassing Elders. Be polite but firm and don't hesitate to intimidate as may be required.

In the meantime, Naomi told Mara, keep close tabs on the mutant in custody. Ensure that she isn't moved and, if possible, facilitate an escape. Naomi encouraged Mara that she could do much more than she thought she could if she just took the gloves off and went bare knuckle with the humans.

Mara thanked Naomi for her advice and said she would start working on the problem immediately. The computer screen dissolved into Kaleidoscope's screen saver mode.

"Well," Naomi thought to herself as she, too headed to bed, "It's been just another day in the life of a Sentinel."

Epilogue

When Red Hawk finished her narrative, she closed her eyes for a moment. To those closest to her it even looked as though she was pausing to regain her strength. Then she looked out over her audience and again paused.

"I know that I have lived through many years of Elder history," she said. "I have been quite fortunate to have been able to look behind the scenes, to talk with many of the major participants in your greatest adventures. I am now feeling my age. We humans do not have your longevity. After seventy – eighty years our bodies just wear out.

"Now, I would like to introduce you to the young man I am training to take my place. Please meet, White Wolf, a descendant of Grey Wolf's clan."

While all eyes had been on Red Hawk, a young Indian man had surreptitiously entered the Valley behind her. He now walked up beside her and stood silently. He had a lithe body, well muscled, and black hair. He was wearing a head band similar to the one Red Hawk always wore, a deer-skin breechclout and moccasins. He also had a sheath knife hanging from the belt about his waist. He had evidently not yet earned his medicine bag, for it was missing.

The Elders stared at the new arrival most undiplomatically. It hardly occurred to them that White Wolf was staring right back at the Elders.

After a couple of minutes of mutual staring, Red Hawk intervened.

"I will continue my lessons for as long as I am able. White Wolf has almost completed his training. As soon as he is appointed as the tribal shaman, he will be taking over Grey Wolf's cabin and will be your primary contact and protector, for as long as you may need his services."

With that Red Hawk rose, still leaning heavily on her totem stick, and she and White Wolf left the area and exited the Valley.

As Red Hawk left the Valley, Ari-Alla, the Chief Councilor, rose to address the assembled Elders.

"Let me fill you in on the latest news", she said, "directly from Naomi and Serina and the other Sentinels.

"First, the President's executive order has been completely disseminated and all applicable personnel in the Executive Branch have certified their acknowledgment of it.

"Second, the Chief of Police in Washington has not only prohibited any further hassling of Elders in the area, she has also been on the lookout for Elders wandering around the District and has established a means of contacting Naomi and Serina so that they might provide any necessary assistance. It is unknown whether her successors will continue the process, but Naomi and Serina are encouraged. This possibility is being explored elsewhere on a tentative basis.

"Red Hawk mentioned Mara in Atlanta. She was unable to free the seized Elder by herself, so Lila, an expert in electronics, went to Atlanta to help her out. Working together, they were able to free the young Elder and fill her in on her history. Lila liked Atlanta so much, that she decided to stick around and team up with Mara. I think they are going to make an excellent team.

"As a result of these actions, the Council has made it a rule to always appoint two sentinels to each posting. Other adepts have been asked to fill in wherever only a single sentinel had been assigned. So far the results have been excellent.

"At the present time, we feel entirely secure here in the Valley. There are no longer any known or suspected hazards. So let us celebrate this momentous occasion in true Elder fashion: Let there be a party!"

== 30 ==

Also by Robyn Kelly:

Watch for volume nine

The Elder Chronicles: Armageddon

Coming Soon!

www.ingramcontent.com/pod-product-compliance
Lightning Source LLC
Chambersburg PA
CBHW030643130626
46552CB00002B/987